# Mr Gilfil's Love Story

George Eliot

ET REMOTISSIMA PROPE

Hesperus Classics

Hesperus Classics
Published by Hesperus Press Limited
4 Rickett Street, London sw6 1ru
www.hesperuspress.com

First published in *Blackwood's Edinburgh Magazine* in 1857; published together
with 'Amos Barton' and 'Janet's Repentance' as *Scenes of Clerical Life* in 1858.
First published by Hesperus Press Limited, 2006

Foreword © Kirsty Gunn, 2006

Designed and typeset by Fraser Muggeridge studio
Printed in Jordan by the Jordan National Press

isbn: 1-84391-142-6
isbn13: 978-184391-142-5

# CONTENTS

# FOREWORD

The fictional world of George Eliot is a deeply and richly domestic place. Described by community, social norms and familiar codes of behaviour, how distinctive, how appealing it is, how it satisfies. When we visit the sites of other novels of her period we see George Eliot's stories are self-contained by comparison, using everything within them to create a multifunctioning and complex narrative. Where other books must reach out to the world of adventure, plot and intrigues that rely on outsiders and outside information to give them buzz and energy, Eliot's are stories built on home ground. Here is the local village, the small town.

'When old Mr Gilfil died' begins the story we have here, 'thirty years ago, there was general sorrow in Shepperton…' Right from the beginning it's clear that in *Mr Gilfil's Love Story* we're going to feel as familiar with the characters and the situation of a plot as a neighbour or friend might – Shepperton could be just down the road, 'old Mr Gilfil' sounds with affection and length of acquaintance.

*Mr Gilfil's Love Story* is just that, a tale of the heart that unfolds in reverse – opening with a portrait of someone who you would have thought has always been a bachelor, Maynard Gilfil as an old man, kindly, generous, with pockets full of sweeties for the local children – and then going back into the past to relate his love for an Italian orphan who came to live and grow up in the house of his benefactor.

In so many ways the story, like the length of the book itself, is slight: Gilfil's love is unrequited then met; the object of his affections has feelings for another man, these change. Yet the whole thing aches with human aspirations and hope – all the feelings of Eliot's much longer books gathered up and beautifully contained here. In fact, it is the very compression of this book that makes it interesting in ways that are apart from the usual satisfactions of those other novels, Eliot pointing us, quite deliberately, I think, towards a way of reading that sums up situations fast and moves on, to show us that the domestic subject that is quietly present in all her books, behind the subtle details of those slower moving dramas, is in fact her overriding theme.

She does this by creating a story that seems to undermine itself, as though we are not meant to take the main narrative at face value at all.

We notice it first in the straightforward appropriation of the love story as subject – there's much in *Mr Gilfil's Love Story* that can remind us of something like *Bridget Jones's Diary*, bitchy, frank, funny in parts and quite hard to take seriously. Caterina, or Tina as she's known, bares her feelings liberally, lets herself go. And all because she's in love with someone who doesn't love her. How modern this seems, the blatant preoccupation with self, how shallow – yet in fact there is something of the adolescent in most of the characters Eliot has created here: Sir Christopher, the kindly but pompous father figure, blithely proposing marriages as though they were the easiest contract in the world to negotiate and remaining blind to the reality of relationships as they really are; the affianced and priggish Miss Assher and her boring mother who 'refreshed by a doze… was in great force for monologue'. There's Wybrow, the caddish, jilting lover who takes long self-satisfied looks at himself in the mirror; there's old faithful Bates the gardener, crouched by the fire in his gnomish home. None of them are meant to be thoroughly realistic, not in the way Eliot makes characters in her other books real. They are almost cartoon-like by comparison (their very names enough to suggest it), drawn as parts, not wholes. Sir Christopher appears more often than not as his shirt and waistcoat front, Wybrow as his continuous flop of soft hair. Our heroine is a 'clever black-eyed monkey', as her adoptive father calls her, or later a little tendril 'put[ting] up her little mouth to be kissed'.

Only Maynard Gilfil himself resists this kind of description – and that's because he's barely described at all. His invisibility, to Tina, to her father, and to us the reader… This is the one element of the story that moves us, lifts us. For his love, too, is invisible. In the way she has centred the book around absence, a love not recognised, a character who seems invisible, George Eliot makes her story more modern than by simply creating a contemporary-feeling plot. It becomes modern in literary terms. In the end, *Mr Gilfil's Love Story*, despite all its girlish preoccupations, resonates more with Ford Madox Ford's *The Good Soldier* than anything Helen Fielding may have fashioned.

So it's complicated then, this compressed little story. And in addition to these complications – the told against the untold story, the garishness of the cartoon character set beside the quiet, effaced individual – Eliot extends herself further. For *Mr Gilfil's Love Story* is also just plain weird. There's a strange gothic element at work in the book that overcharges certain scenes with drama, lending a feverish, melodramatic atmosphere that seems at odds with the classic Englishness of the story. As a child in Italy playing next to her dying father's bed, Tina's 'large dark eyes shone from out her queer little face, like two precious stones in a grotesque image carved in old ivory'; much later she lies tossing on her bed in England and the same dark, hectic mood persists. The measured domestic familiarity is freaked by these details and by strange twists in the plot: a lover found dead in a pile of leaves, a fiendish dagger taken from the wall. This is not to say that Eliot's bigger novels don't contain drama on a certain scale – but here, in the forced atmosphere of the short novel, it seems more extreme and strange. And how odd to have the author of tact and felicity, who leaves her other books all open to the reader's subtlety of interpretation, here rushing about this way: 'Her heart throbs as if it would burst her bosom – as if every next leap must be its last. Wait, wait, O heart! – till she has done this one deed.'

Yet again I would say it's the concentrated nature of this particular book that gives Eliot a way of championing her larger literary ambitions, present in all her work but never as obvious as here: to portray the extraordinary fact of ordinary life, to show the rich variety that is present in the domestic subject. At the end of the day, Eliot is saying, like Chekhov, with whom she shares a method of setting the outlandish alongside the mundane, Life Goes On. Maynard Gilfil, dead thirty years at the beginning of this story, lived out his quiet existence with no one having any sense of the drama he was once witness to, the love he was once able to satisfy. Yet from that quietness George Eliot has made something that sounds long after we have finished reading: a love story that would have seemed to have been invisible to the world in the way ordinary life can so often seem to be invisible… Brought out here for all of us to see.

*– Kirsty Gunn, 2006*

# Mr Gilfil's Love Story

When old Mr Gilfil died, thirty years ago, there was general sorrow in Shepperton, and if black cloth had not been hung round the pulpit and reading-desk, by order of his nephew and principal legatee, the parishioners would certainly have subscribed the necessary sum out of their own pockets, rather than allow such a tribute of respect to be wanting. All the farmers' wives brought out their black bombazines, and Mrs Jennings, at the Wharf, by appearing the first Sunday after Mr Gilfil's death in her salmon-coloured ribbons and green shawl, excited the severest remark. To be sure, Mrs Jennings was a newcomer, and town-bred, so that she could hardly be expected to have very clear notions of what was proper, but, as Mrs Higgins observed in an undertone to Mrs Parrot when they were coming out of church, 'Her husband, who'd been born i' the parish, might ha' told her better.' An unreadiness to put on black on all available occasions, or too great an alacrity in putting it off, argued, in Mrs Higgins' opinion, a dangerous levity of character, and an unnatural insensibility to the essential fitness of things.

'Some folks can't a-bear to put off their colours,' she remarked; 'but that was never the way i' *my* family. Why, Mrs Parrot, from the time I was married, till Mr Higgins died, nine years ago come Candlemas, I niver was out o' black two year together!'

'Ah,' said Mrs Parrot, who was conscious of inferiority in this respect, 'there isn't many families as have had so many deaths as yours, Mrs Higgins.'

Mrs Higgins, who was an elderly widow, 'well left', reflected with complacency that Mrs Parrot's observation was no more than just, and that Mrs Jennings very likely belonged to a family that had had no funerals to speak of.

Even dirty Dame Fripp, who was a very rare church-goer, had been to Mrs Hackit to beg a bit of old crape, and with this sign of grief pinned on her little coal-scuttle bonnet, was seen dropping her curtsy opposite the reading-desk. This manifestation of respect towards Mr Gilfil's memory on the part of Dame Fripp had no theological bearing whatever. It was due to an event that had occurred some years back, and which, I am sorry to say, had left that grimy old lady as indifferent to the means of grace as ever. Dame Fripp kept leeches, and was understood to have such remarkable influence over those wilful animals in inducing them to bite under the most unpromising circumstances, that though her own leeches were usually rejected, from a suspicion that they had lost their appetite, she herself was constantly called in to apply the more lively individuals furnished from Mr Pilgrim's surgery, when, as was very often the case, one of that clever man's paying patients was attacked with inflammation. Thus Dame Fripp, in addition to 'property' supposed to yield her no less than half-a-crown a week, was in the receipt of professional fees, the gross amount of which was vaguely estimated by her neighbours as 'pouns an' pouns'. Moreover, she drove a brisk trade in lollipop with epicurean urchins, who recklessly purchased that luxury at the rate of two hundred per cent. Nevertheless, with all these notorious sources of income, the shameless old woman constantly pleaded poverty, and begged for scraps at Mrs Hackit's, who, though she always said Mrs Fripp was 'as false as two folks', and no better than a miser and a heathen, had yet a leaning towards her as an old neighbour.

'There's that case-hardened old Judy a-coming after the tea leaves again,' Mrs Hackit would say; 'an' I'm fool enough to give 'em her, though Sally wants 'em all the while to sweep the floors with!'

Such was Dame Fripp, whom Mr Gilfil, riding leisurely in top boots and spurs from doing duty at Knebley one warm Sunday afternoon, observed sitting in the dry ditch near her cottage, and by her side a large pig, who, with that ease and confidence belonging to perfect friendship, was lying with his head in her lap, and making no effort to play the agreeable beyond an occasional grunt.

'Why, Mrs Fripp,' said the vicar, 'I didn't know you had such a fine pig. You'll have some rare flitches at Christmas!'

'Eh, God forbid! My son gev him me two 'ear ago, an' he's been company to me iver sin'. I couldn't find i' my heart to part wi'm, if I niver knowed the taste o' bacon-fat again.'

'Why, he'll eat his head off, and yours too. How can you go on keeping a pig, and making nothing by him?'

4

'O, he picks a bit hisself wi' rootin', and I dooant mind doing wi'out to gi' him summat. A bit o' company's meat an' drink too, an' he follers me about, and grunts when I spake to'm, just like a Christian.'

Mr Gilfil laughed, and I am obliged to admit that he said goodbye to Dame Fripp without asking her why she had not been to church, or making the slightest effort for her spiritual edification. But the next day he ordered his man David to take her a great piece of bacon, with a message, saying, the parson wanted to make sure that Mrs Fripp would know the taste of bacon-fat again. So, when Mr Gilfil died, Dame Fripp manifested her gratitude and reverence in the simply dingy fashion I have mentioned.

You already suspect that the vicar did not shine in the more spiritual functions of his office, and indeed, the utmost I can say for him in this respect is, that he performed those functions with undeviating attention to brevity and despatch. He had a large heap of short sermons, rather yellow and worn at the edges, from which he took two every Sunday, securing perfect impartiality in the selection by taking them as they came, without reference to topics, and having preached one of these sermons at Shepperton in the morning, he mounted his horse and rode hastily with the other in his pocket to Knebley, where he officiated in a wonderful little church, with a checkered pavement that had once rung to the iron tread of military monks, with coats of arms in clusters on the lofty roof, marble warriors and their wives without noses occupying a large proportion of the area, and the twelve apostles, with their heads very much on one side, holding didactic ribbons, painted in fresco on the walls. Here, in an absence of mind to which he was prone, Mr Gilfil would sometimes forget to take off his spurs before putting on his surplice, and only become aware of the omission by feeling something mysteriously tugging at the skirts of that garment as he stepped into the reading-desk. But the Knebley farmers would as soon have thought of criticising the moon as their pastor. He belonged to the course of nature, like markets and toll gates and dirty banknotes, and being a vicar, his claim on their veneration had never been counteracted by an exasperating claim on their pockets. Some of them, who did not indulge in the superfluity of a covered cart without springs, had dined half an hour earlier than usual – that is to say, at twelve o'clock – in order to have time for their long walk through miry lanes, and present themselves duly in their places at two o'clock, when Mr Oldinport and Lady Felicia, to whom Knebley Church was a sort of family temple, made their way among the bows and curtsies of their dependants to a carved and canopied pew in the chancel, diffusing as they went a delicate odour of Indian roses on the unsusceptible nostrils of the congregation.

The farmers' wives and children sat on the dark oaken benches, but the husbands usually chose the distinctive dignity of a stall under one of the twelve apostles, where, when the alternation of prayers and responses had given place to the agreeable monotony of the sermon, Paterfamilias might be seen or heard sinking into a pleasant doze, from which he infallibly woke up at the sound of the concluding doxology. And then they made their way back again through the miry lanes, perhaps almost as much the better for this simple weekly tribute to what they knew of good and right, as many a more wakeful and critical congregation of the present day.

Mr Gilfil, too, used to make his way home in the later years of his life, for he had given up the habit of dining at Knebley Abbey on a Sunday, having, I am sorry to say, had a very bitter quarrel with Mr Oldinport, the cousin and predecessor of the Mr Oldinport who flourished in the Revd Amos Barton's time. That quarrel was a sad pity, for the two had had many a good day's hunting together when they were younger, and in those friendly times not a few members of the hunt envied Mr Oldinport the excellent terms he was on with his vicar, for, as Sir Jasper Sitwell observed, 'next to a man's wife, there's nobody can be such an infernal plague to you as a parson, always under your nose on your own estate.'

I fancy the original difference which led to the rupture was very slight, but Mr Gilfil was of an extremely caustic turn, his satire having a flavour of originality that was quite wanting in his sermons; and as Mr Oldinport's armour of conscious virtue presented some considerable and conspicuous gaps, the vicar's keen-edged retorts probably made a few incisions too deep to be forgiven. Such, at least, was the view of the case presented by Mr Hackit, who knew as much of the matter as any third person. For, the very week after the quarrel, when presiding at the annual dinner of the Association for the Prosecution of Felons, held at the Oldinport Arms, he contributed an additional zest to the conviviality on that occasion by informing the company that 'the parson had given the squire a lick with the rough side of his tongue'. The detection of the person or persons who had driven off Mr Parrot's heifer, could hardly have been more welcome news to the Shepperton tenantry, with whom Mr Oldinport was in the worst odour as a land-lord, having kept up his rents in spite of falling prices, and not being in the least stung to emulation by paragraphs in the provincial news-papers, stating that the Honourable Augustus Purwell, or Viscount Blethers, had made a return of ten per cent on their last rent-day. The fact was, Mr Oldinport had not the slightest intention of standing for Parliament, whereas he had the strongest intention of adding to his unentailed estate. Hence, to the Shepperton farmers it was as good as lemon with their grog to know that the vicar had thrown out sarcasms against the squire's charities, as little better than those of the man who stole a goose, and gave away the giblets in alms. For Shepperton, you observe, was in a state of Attic culture compared with Knebley; it had turnpike roads and a public opinion, whereas, in the Boeotian Knebley,[1] men's minds and waggons alike moved in the deepest of ruts, and the landlord was only grumbled at as a necessary and unalterable evil, like the weather, the weevils, and the turnip-fly.

Thus in Shepperton this breach with Mr Oldinport tended only to heighten that good understanding that the vicar had always enjoyed with the rest of his parishioners, from the generation whose children he had christened a quarter of a century before, down to that hope-ful generation represented by little Tommy Bond, who had recently quitted frocks and trousers for the severe simplicity of a tight suit of corduroys, relieved by numerous brass buttons. Tommy was a saucy boy, impervious to all impressions of reverence, and excessively addicted to humming-tops and marbles, with which recreative re-sources he was in the habit of immoderately distending the pockets of his corduroys. One day, spinning his top on the garden-walk, and seeing the vicar advance directly towards it, at that exciting moment when it was beginning to 'sleep' magnificently, he shouted out with all the force of his lungs – 'Stop! don't knock my top down, now!'

From that day 'little Corduroys' had been an especial favourite with Mr Gilfil, who delighted to provoke his ready scorn and wonder by putting questions that gave Tommy the meanest opinion of his intellect.

'Well, little Corduroys, have they milked the geese today?'

'Milked the geese! why, they don't milk the geese, you silly!'

'No! dear heart! why, how do the goslings live, then?'

The nutriment of goslings rather transcending Tommy's observations in natural history, he feigned to understand this question in an exclamatory rather than an interrogatory sense, and became absorbed in winding up his top.

'Ah, I see you don't know how the goslings live! But did you notice how it rained sugarplums yesterday?' (Here Tommy became attentive.) 'Why, they fell into my pocket as I rode along. You look in my pocket and see if they didn't.' Tommy, without waiting to discuss the alleged antecedent, lost no time in ascertaining the presence of the agreeable consequent, for he had a well-founded belief in the advantages of diving into the vicar's pocket. Mr Gilfil called it his wonderful pocket, because, as he delighted to tell the 'young shavers' and 'two-shoes' – so he called all little boys and girls – whenever he put pennies into it, they turned into sugarplums or gingerbread, or some other nice thing. Indeed, little Bessie Parrot, a flaxen-headed 'two-shoes', very white and fat as to her neck, always had the admirable directness and sincerity to salute him with the question – 'What zoo dot in zoo pottet?'

You can imagine, then, that the christening dinners were none the less merry for the presence of the parson. The farmers relished his society particularly, for he could not only smoke his pipe, and season the details of parish affairs with abundance of caustic jokes and proverbs, but, as Mr Bond often said, no man knew more than the vicar about the breed of cows and horses. He had grazing-land of his own about five miles off, which a bailiff, ostensibly a tenant, farmed under his direction, and to ride backwards and forwards, and look after the buying and selling of stock, was the old gentleman's chief relaxation, now his hunting days were over. To hear him discussing the respective merits of the Devonshire breed and the shorthorns, or the last foolish decision of the magistrates about a pauper, a superficial observer might have seen little difference, beyond his superior shrewdness, between the vicar and his bucolic parishioners, for it was his habit to approximate his accent and mode of speech to theirs, doubtless because he thought it a mere frustration of the purposes of language to talk of 'shear-hogs'[2] and 'ewes' to men who habitually said 'sharrags' and 'yowes'. Nevertheless the farmers themselves were perfectly aware of the distinction between them and the parson, and had not at all the less belief in him as a gentleman and a clergyman for his easy speech and familiar manners. Mrs Parrot smoothed her apron and set her cap right with the utmost solicitude when she saw the vicar coming, made him her deepest curtsy, and every Christmas had a fat turkey ready to send him with her 'duty'. And in the most gossiping colloquies with Mr Gilfil, you might have observed that both men and women 'minded their words', and never became indifferent to his approbation.

The same respect attended him in his strictly clerical functions. The benefits of baptism were supposed to be somehow bound up with Mr Gilfil's personality, so metaphysical a distinction as that between a man and his office being, as yet, quite foreign to the mind of a good Shepperton Churchman, savouring, he would have thought, of Dissent on the very face of it. Miss Selina Parrot put off her marriage a whole month when Mr Gilfil had an attack of rheumatism, rather than be married in a makeshift manner by the Milby curate.

'We've had a very good sermon this morning', was the frequent remark, after hearing one of the old yellow series, heard with all the more satisfaction because it had been heard for the twentieth time, for to minds on the Shepperton level it is repetition, not novelty, that produces the strongest effect, and phrases, like tunes, are a long time making themselves at home in the brain.

Mr Gilfil's sermons, as you may imagine, were not of a highly doctrinal, still less of a polemical, cast. They perhaps did not search the conscience very powerfully, for you remember that to Mrs Patten, who had listened to them thirty years, the announcement that she was a sinner appeared an uncivil heresy, but, on the other hand, they made no unreasonable demand on the Shepperton intellect – amounting, indeed, to little more than an expansion of the concise thesis, that those who do wrong will find it the worse for them, and those who do well will find it the better for them; the nature of wrongdoing being exposed in special sermons against lying, backbiting, anger, slothfulness, and the like; and welldoing being interpreted as honesty, truthfulness, charity, industry, and other common virtues, lying quite on the surface of life, and having very little to do with deep spiritual doctrine. Mrs Patten understood that if she turned out ill-crushed cheeses, a just retribution awaited her; though, I fear, she made no particular application of the sermon on backbiting. Mrs Hackit expressed herself greatly edified by the sermon on honesty, the allusion to the unjust weight and deceitful balance having a peculiar lucidity for her, owing to a recent dispute with her grocer, but I am not aware that she ever appeared to be much struck by the sermon on anger.

As to any suspicion that Mr Gilfil did not dispense the pure Gospel, or any strictures on his doctrine and mode of delivery, such thoughts never visited the minds of the Shepperton parishioners – of those very parishioners who, ten or fifteen years later, showed themselves extremely critical of Mr Barton's discourses and demeanour. But in the interim they had tasted that dangerous fruit of the tree of knowledge – innovation that is well known to open the eyes, even in an uncomfortable manner. At present, to find fault with the sermon was regarded as almost equivalent to finding fault with religion itself. One Sunday, Mr Hackit's nephew, Master Tom Stokes, a flippant town youth, greatly scandalised his excellent relatives by declaring that he could write as good a sermon as Mr Gilfil's; whereupon Mr Hackit sought to reduce the presumptuous youth to utter confusion, by offering him a sovereign if he would fulfil his vaunt. The sermon was written, however, and though it was not admitted to be anywhere within reach of Mr Gilfil's, it was yet so astonishingly like a sermon, having a text, three divisions, and a concluding exhortation beginning 'And now, my brethren', that the sovereign, though denied formally, was bestowed informally, and the sermon was pronounced, when Master Stokes's back was turned, to be 'an uncommon cliver thing'.

The Revd Mr Pickard, indeed, of the Independent Meeting, had stated, in a sermon preached at Rotheby, for the reduction of a debt on New Zion, built, with an exuberance of faith and a deficiency of funds, by seceders from the original Zion, that he lived in a parish where the vicar was very 'dark', and in the prayers he addressed to his own congregation, he was in the habit of comprehensively alluding to the parishioners outside the chapel walls, as those who, 'Gallio-like, cared for none of these things'.[3] But I need hardly say that no church-goer ever came within earshot of Mr Pickard.

It was not to the Shepperton farmers only that Mr Gilfil's society was acceptable; he was a welcome guest at some of the best houses in that part of the country. Old Sir Jasper Sitwell would have been glad to see him every week, and if you had seen him conducting Lady Sitwell in to dinner, or had heard him talking to her with quaint yet graceful gallantry, you would have inferred that the earlier period of his life had been passed in more stately society than could be found in Shepperton, and that his slipshod chat and homely manners were but like weather-stains on a fine old block of marble, allowing you still to see here and there the fineness of the grain, and the delicacy of the original tint. But in his later years these visits became a little too troublesome to the old gentleman, and he was rarely to be found anywhere of an evening beyond the bounds of his own parish – most frequently, indeed, by the side of his own sitting-room fire, smoking his pipe, and maintaining the pleasing antithesis of dryness and moisture by an occasional sip of gin-and-water.

Here I am aware that I have run the risk of alienating all my refined lady-readers, and utterly annihilating any curiosity they may have felt to know the details of Mr Gilfil's love story. 'Gin-and-water! foh! you may as well ask us to interest ourselves in the romance of a tallow-chandler, who mingles the image of his beloved with short dips and moulds.'

But in the first place, dear ladies, allow me to plead that gin-and-water, like obesity, or baldness, or the gout, does not exclude a vast amount of antecedent romance, any more than the neatly executed 'fronts'[4] that you may some day wear, will exclude your present possession of less expensive braids. Alas, alas! we poor mortals are often little better than wood-ashes – there is small sign of the sap, and the leafy freshness, and the bursting buds that were once there; but wherever we see wood-ashes, we know that all that early fullness of life must have been. I, at least, hardly ever look at a bent old man, or a wizened old woman, but I see also, with my mind's eye, that Past of which they are the shrunken remnant, and the unfinished romance of

11

rosy cheeks and bright eyes seems sometimes of feeble interest and significance, compared with that drama of hope and love that has long ago reached its catastrophe, and left the poor soul, like a dim and dusty stage, with all its sweet garden scenes and fair perspectives overturned and thrust out of sight.

In the second place, let me assure you that Mr Gilfil's potations of gin-and-water were quite moderate. His nose was not rubicund; on the contrary, his white hair hung around a pale and venerable face. He drank it chiefly, I believe, because it was cheap, and here I find myself alighting on another of the vicar's weaknesses, which, if I had cared to paint a flattering portrait rather than a faithful one, I might have chosen to suppress. It is undeniable that, as the years advanced, Mr Gilfil became, as Mr Hackit observed, more and more 'close-fisted', though the growing propensity showed itself rather in the parsimony of his personal habits, than in withholding help from the needy. He was saving – so he represented the matter to himself – for a nephew, the only son of a sister who had been the dearest object, all but one, in his life. 'The lad,' he thought, 'will have a nice little fortune to begin life with, and will bring his pretty young wife some day to see the spot where his old uncle lies. It will perhaps be all the better for his hearth that mine was lonely.'

Mr Gilfil was a bachelor, then?

That is the conclusion to which you would probably have come if you had entered his sitting room, where the bare tables, the large old-fashioned horsehair chairs, and the threadbare Turkey carpet perpetually fumigated with tobacco, seemed to tell a story of wifeless existence that was contradicted by no portrait, no piece of embroidery, no faded bit of pretty triviality, hinting of taper-fingers and small feminine ambitions. And it was here that Mr Gilfil passed his evenings, seldom with other society than that of Ponto, his old brown setter, who, stretched out at full length on the rug with his nose between his forepaws, would wrinkle his brows and lift up his eyelids every now and then, to exchange a glance of mutual understanding with his master. But there was a chamber in Shepperton Vicarage that told a different story from that bare and cheerless dining room – a chamber never entered by anyone besides Mr Gilfil and old Martha the housekeeper, who, with David her husband as groom and gardener, formed the vicar's entire establishment. The blinds of this chamber were always down, except once a quarter, when Martha entered that she might air and clean it. She always asked Mr Gilfil for the key, which he kept locked up in his bureau, and returned it to him when she had finished her task.

It was a touching sight that the daylight streamed in upon, as Martha drew aside the blinds and thick curtains, and opened the Gothic casement of the oriel window! On the little dressing table there was a dainty looking glass in a carved and gilt frame; bits of wax-candle were still in the branched sockets at the sides, and on one of these branches hung a little black lace kerchief; a faded satin pincushion, with the pins rusted in it, a scent-bottle, and a large green fan, lay on the table; and on a dressing-box by the side of the glass was a work-basket, and an unfinished baby-cap, yellow with age, lying in it. Two gowns, of a fashion long forgotten, were hanging on nails against the door, and a pair of tiny red slippers, with a bit of tarnished silver embroidery on them, were standing at the foot of the bed. Two or three watercolour drawings, views of Naples, hung upon the walls, and over the mantelpiece, above some bits of rare old china, two miniatures in oval frames. One of these miniatures represented a young man about seven-and-twenty, with a sanguine complexion, full lips, and clear candid grey eyes. The other was the likeness of a girl probably not more than eighteen, with small features, thin cheeks, a pale southern-looking complexion, and large dark eyes. The gentleman wore powder; the lady had her dark hair gathered away from her face, and a little cap, with a cherry-coloured bow, set on the top of her head – a coquettish headdress, but the eyes spoke of sadness rather than of coquetry.

Such were the things that Martha had dusted and let the air upon, four times a year, ever since she was a blooming lass of twenty, and she was now, in this last decade of Mr Gilfil's life, unquestionably on the wrong side of fifty. Such was the locked-up chamber in Mr Gilfil's house: a sort of visible symbol of the secret chamber in his heart, where he had long turned the key on early hopes and early sorrows, shutting up for ever all the passion and the poetry of his life.

There were not many people in the parish, besides Martha, who had any very distinct remembrance of Mr Gilfil's wife, or indeed who knew anything of her, beyond the fact that there was a marble tablet, with a Latin inscription in memory of her, over the vicarage pew. The parishioners who were old enough to remember her arrival were not generally gifted with descriptive powers, and the utmost you could gather from them was, that Mrs Gilfil looked like a 'furriner, wi' such eyes, you can't think, an' a voice as went through you when she sung at church.' The one exception was Mrs Patten, whose strong memory and taste for personal narrative made her a great source of oral tradition in Shepperton. Mr Hackit, who had not come into the parish until ten years after Mrs Gilfil's death, would often put old questions to Mrs Patten for the sake of getting the old answers, which pleased him in the same way as passages from a favourite book, or the scenes of a familiar play, please more accomplished people.

'Ah, you remember well the Sunday as Mrs Gilfil first come to church, eh, Mrs Patten?'

'To be sure I do. It was a fine bright Sunday as ever was seen, just at the beginnin' o' hay harvest. Mr Tarbett preached that day, and Mr Gilfil sat i' the pew with his wife. I think I see him now, a-leading her up the aisle, an' her head not reachin' much above his elber: a little pale woman, with eyes as black as sloes, an' yet lookin' blank-like, as if she see'd nothing with 'em.'

'I warrant she had her weddin' clothes on?' said Mr Hackit.

'Nothin' partikler smart – on'y a white hat tied down under her chin, an' a white Indy muslin gown. But you don't know what Mr Gilfil was in those times. He was fine an' altered before you come into the parish. He'd a fresh colour then, an' a bright look wi' his eyes, as did your heart good to see. He looked rare and happy that Sunday; but somehow, I'd a feelin' as it wouldn't last long. I've no opinion o' furriners, Mr Hackit, for I've travelled i' their country with my lady in my time, an' seen enough o' their victuals an' their nasty ways.'

'Mrs Gilfil come from It'ly, didn't she?'

'I reckon she did, but I niver could rightly hear about that. Mr Gilfil was niver to be spoke to about her, and nobody else hereabout knowed anythin'. Howiver, she must ha' come over pretty young, for she spoke

English as well as you an' me. It's them Italians as has such fine voices, an' Mrs Gilfil sung, you never heared the like. He brought her here to have tea with me one afternoon, and says he, in his jovial way, "Now, Mrs Patten, I want Mrs Gilfil to see the neatest house, and drink the best cup o' tea, in all Shepperton; you must show her your dairy and your cheese room, and then she shall sing you a song." An' so she did; an' her voice seemed sometimes to fill the room; an' then it went low an' soft, as if it was whisperin' close to your heart like.'

'You never heared her again, I reckon?'

'No; she was sickly then, and she died in a few months after. She wasn't in the parish much more nor half a year altogether. She didn't seem lively that afternoon, an' I could see she didn't care about the dairy, nor the cheeses, on'y she pretended, to please him. As for him, I niver see'd a man so wrapt up in a woman. He looked at her as if he was worshippin' her, an' as if he wanted to lift her off the ground ivery minute, to save her the trouble o' walkin'. Poor man, poor man! It had like to ha' killed him when she died, though he niver gev way, but went on ridin' about and preachin'. But he was wore to a shadder, an' his eyes used to look as dead – you wouldn't ha' knowed 'em.'

'She brought him no fortune?'

'Not she. All Mr Gilfil's property come by his mother's side. There was blood an' money too, there. It's a thousand pities as he married i' that way – a fine man like him, as might ha' had the pick o' the county, an' had his grandchildren about him now. An' him so fond o' children, too.'

In this manner Mrs Patten usually wound up her reminiscences of the vicar's wife, of whom, you perceive, she knew but little. It was clear that the communicative old lady had nothing to tell of Mrs Gilfil's history previous to her arrival in Shepperton, and that she was unacquainted with Mr Gilfil's love story.

But I, dear reader, am quite as communicative as Mrs Patten, and much better informed; so that, if you care to know more about the vicar's courtship and marriage, you need only carry your imagination back to the latter end of the last century, and your attention forward into the next chapter.

## 2

It is the evening of the 21st of June 1788. The day has been bright and sultry, and the sun will still be more than an hour above the horizon, but his rays, broken by the leafy fretwork of the elms that border the park, no longer prevent two ladies from carrying out their cushions and embroidery, and seating themselves to work on the lawn in front of Cheverel Manor. The soft turf gives way even under the fairy tread of the younger lady, whose small stature and slim figure rest on the tiniest of full-grown feet. She trips along before the elder, carrying the cushions, which she places in the favourite spot, just on the slope by a clump of laurels, where they can see the sunbeams sparkling among the water lilies, and can be themselves seen from the dining-room windows. She has deposited the cushions, and now turns round, so that you may have a full view of her as she stands waiting the slower advance of the elder lady. You are at once arrested by her large dark eyes, which, in their inexpressive unconscious beauty, resemble the eyes of a fawn, and it is only by an effort of attention that you notice the absence of bloom on her young cheek, and the southern yellowish tint of her small neck and face, rising above the little black lace kerchief that prevents the too immediate comparison of her skin with her white muslin gown. Her large eyes seem all the more striking because the dark hair is gathered away from her face, under a little cap set at the top of her head, with a cherry-coloured bow on one side.

The elder lady, who is advancing towards the cushions, is cast in a very different mould of womanhood. She is tall, and looks the taller because her powdered hair is turned backward over a toupee, and surmounted by lace and ribbons. She is nearly fifty, but her complexion is still fresh and beautiful, with the beauty of an auburn blond; her proud pouting lips, and her head thrown a little backward as she walks, give an expression of hauteur that is not contradicted by the cold grey eye. The tucked-in kerchief, rising full over the low tight bodice of her blue dress, sets off the majestic form of her bust, and she treads the lawn as if she were one of Sir Joshua Reynolds'[5] stately ladies, who had suddenly stepped from her frame to enjoy the evening cool.

'Put the cushions lower, Caterina, that we may not have so much sun upon us,' she called out, in a tone of authority, when still at some distance. Caterina obeyed, and they sat down, making two bright patches of red and white and blue on the green background of the laurels and the lawn, which would look none the less pretty in a picture because one of the women's hearts was rather cold and the other rather sad.

And a charming picture Cheverel Manor would have made that evening, if some English Watteau[6] had been there to paint it: the castellated house of grey-tinted stone, with the flickering sunbeams sending dashes of golden light across the many-shaped panes in the mullioned windows, and a great beech leaning athwart one of the flanking towers, and breaking, with its dark flattened boughs, the too formal symmetry of the front; the broad gravel walk winding on the right, by a row of tall pines, alongside the pool – on the left branching out among swelling grassy mounds, surmounted by clumps of trees, where the red trunk of the Scotch fir glows in the descending sunlight against the bright green of limes and acacias; the great pool, where a pair of swans are swimming lazily with one leg tucked under a wing, and where the open water lilies lie calmly accepting the kisses of the fluttering light-sparkles; the lawn, with its smooth emerald greenness, sloping down to the rougher and browner herbage of the park, from which it is invisibly fenced by a little stream that winds away from the pool, and disappears under a wooden bridge in the distant pleasure-ground; and on this lawn our two ladies, whose part in the landscape the painter, standing at a favourable point of view in the park, would represent with a few little dabs of red and white and blue.

Seen from the great Gothic windows of the dining room, they had much more definiteness of outline, and were distinctly visible to the three gentlemen sipping their claret there, as two fair women in whom all three had a personal interest. These gentlemen were a group worth considering attentively, but anyone entering that dining room for the first time would perhaps have had his attention even more strongly arrested by the room itself, which was so bare of furniture that it impressed one with its architectural beauty like a cathedral. A piece of matting stretched from door to door, a bit of worn carpet under the dining table, and a sideboard in a deep recess, did not detain the eye for a moment from the lofty groined ceiling, with its richly carved pendants, all of creamy white, relieved here and there by touches of gold. On one side, this lofty ceiling was supported by pillars and arches, beyond which a lower ceiling, a miniature copy of the higher one, covered the square projection that, with its three large pointed windows, formed the central feature of the building. The room looked less like a place to dine in than a piece of space enclosed simply for the sake of beautiful outline, and the small dining table, with the party round it, seemed an odd and insignificant accident, rather than any-thing connected with the original purpose of the apartment.

But, examined closely, that group was far from insignificant, for the eldest, who was reading in the newspaper the last portentous proceed-ings of the French parliaments, and turning with occasional comments to his young companions, was as fine a specimen of the old English gentleman as could well have been found in those venerable days of cocked hats and pigtails. His dark eyes sparkled under projecting brows, made more prominent by bushy grizzled eyebrows; but any apprehension of severity excited by these penetrating eyes, and by a somewhat aquiline nose, was allayed by the good-natured lines about the mouth, which retained all its teeth and its vigour of expression in spite of sixty winters. The forehead sloped a little from the projecting brows, and its peaked outline was made conspicuous by the arrange-ment of the profusely powdered hair, drawn backward and gathered into a pigtail. He sat in a small hard chair, which did not admit the slightest approach to a lounge, and which showed to advantage the flatness of his back and the breadth of his chest. In fact, Sir Christopher Cheverel was a splendid old gentleman, as anyone may see who enters the saloon at Cheverel Manor, where his full-length portrait, taken when he was fifty, hangs side by side with that of his wife, the stately lady seated on the lawn.

Looking at Sir Christopher, you would at once have been inclined to hope that he had a full-grown son and heir, but perhaps you would have wished that it might not prove to be the young man on his right hand, in whom a certain resemblance to the Baronet, in the contour of the nose and brow, seemed to indicate a family relationship. If this young man had been less elegant in his person, he would have been remarked for the elegance of his dress. But the perfections of his slim well-proportioned figure were so striking that no one but a tailor could notice the perfections of his velvet coat, and his small white hands, with their blue veins and taper fingers, quite eclipsed the beauty of his lace ruffles. The face, however – it was difficult to say why – was certainly not pleasing. Nothing could be more delicate than the blond complexion – its bloom set off by the powdered hair – than the veined overhanging eyelids, which gave an indolent expression to the hazel eyes; nothing more finely cut than the transparent nostril and the short upper lip. Perhaps the chin and lower jaw were too small for an irreproachable profile, but the defect was on the side of that delicacy and finesse that was the distinctive characteristic of the whole person, and which was carried out in the clear brown arch of the eyebrows, and the marble smoothness of the sloping forehead. Impossible to say that this face was not eminently handsome; yet, for the majority both of men and women, it was destitute of charm. Women disliked eyes that seemed to be indolently accepting admiration instead of rendering it, and men, especially if they had a tendency to clumsiness in the nose and ankles, were inclined to think this Antinous[7] in a pigtail a 'confounded puppy'. I fancy that was frequently the inward interjection of the Revd Maynard Gilfil, who was seated on the opposite side of the dining table, though Mr Gilfil's legs and profile were not at all of a kind to make him peculiarly alive to the impertinence and frivolity of personal advantages. His healthy open face and robust limbs were after an excellent pattern for everyday wear, and, in the opinion of Mr Bates, the north-country gardener, would have become regimentals 'a fain saight' better than the 'peaky' features and slight form of Captain Wybrow, notwithstanding that this young gentleman, as Sir Christopher's nephew and destined heir, had the strongest hereditary claim on the gardener's respect, and was undeniably 'clean limbed'. But alas! human longings are perversely obstinate, and to the man whose mouth is watering for a peach, it is of no use to offer the largest vegetable marrow. Mr Gilfil was not sensitive to Mr Bates's opinion, whereas he was sensitive to the opinion of another person, who by no means shared Mr Bates's preference.

Who the other person was it would not have required a very keen observer to guess, from a certain eagerness in Mr Gilfil's glance as that little figure in white tripped along the lawn with the cushions. Captain Wybrow, too, was looking in the same direction, but his handsome face remained handsome – and nothing more.

'Ah,' said Sir Christopher, looking up from his paper, 'there's my lady. Ring for coffee, Anthony; we'll go and join her, and the little monkey Tina shall give us a song.'

The coffee presently appeared, brought not as usual by the footman, in scarlet and drab, but by the old butler, in threadbare but well-brushed black, who, as he was placing it on the table, said – 'If you please, Sir Christopher, there's the widow Hartopp a-crying i' the still room, and begs leave to see your honour.'

'I have given Markham full orders about the widow Hartopp,' said Sir Christopher, in a sharp decided tone. 'I have nothing to say to her.'

'Your honour,' pleaded the butler, rubbing his hands, and putting on an additional coating of humility, 'the poor woman's dreadful over-come, and says she can't sleep a wink this blessed night without seeing your honour, and she begs you to pardon the great freedom she's took to come at this time. She cries fit to break her heart.'

'Ay, ay; water pays no tax. Well, show her into the library.'

Coffee despatched, the two young men walked out through the open window, and joined the ladies on the lawn, while Sir Christopher made his way to the library, solemnly followed by Rupert, his pet bloodhound, who, in his habitual place at the Baronet's right hand, behaved with great urbanity during dinner; but when the cloth was drawn, invariably disappeared under the table, apparently regarding the claret-jug as a mere human weakness, which he winked at, but refused to sanction.

The library lay but three steps from the dining room, on the other side of a cloistered and matted passage. The oriel window was over-shadowed by the great beech, and this, with the flat heavily carved ceiling and the dark hue of the old books that lined the walls, made the room look sombre, especially on entering it from the dining room, with its aerial curves and cream-coloured fretwork touched with gold. As Sir Christopher opened the door, a jet of brighter light fell on a woman in a widow's dress, who stood in the middle of the room, and made the deepest of curtsies as he entered. She was a buxom woman approaching forty, her eyes red with the tears that had evidently been absorbed by the handkerchief gathered into a damp ball in her right hand.

'Now, Mrs Hartopp,' said Sir Christopher, taking out his gold snuff-box and tapping the lid, 'what have you to say to me? Markham has delivered you a notice to quit, I suppose?'

'O yis, your honour, an' that's the reason why I've come. I hope your honour'll think better on it, an' not turn me an' my poor children out o' the farm, where my husband al'ys paid his rent as reglar as the day come.'

'Nonsense! I should like to know what good it will do you and your children to stay on a farm and lose every farthing your husband has left you, instead of selling your stock and going into some little place where you can keep your money together. It is very well known to every tenant of mine that I never allow widows to stay on their husbands' farms.'

'O, Sir Christifer, if you *would* consider – when I've sold the hay, an' corn, an' all the live things, an' paid the debts, an' put the money out to use, I shall have hardly enough to keep our souls an' bodies together. An' how can I rear my boys and put 'em 'prentice? They must go for dey labourers, an' their father a man wi' as good belongings as any on your honour's estate, an' niver threshed his wheat afore it was well i' the rick, nor sold the straw off his farm, nor nothin'. Ask all the farmers round if there was a stiddier, soberer man than my husband as attended Ripstone market. An' he says, "Bessie," says he – them was his last words – "you'll mek a shift to manage the farm, if Sir Christifer 'ull let you stay on."'

'Pooh, pooh!' said Sir Christopher, Mrs Hartopp's sobs having interrupted her pleadings, 'now listen to me, and try to understand a little common sense. You are about as able to manage the farm as your best milch cow. You'll be obliged to have some managing man, who will either cheat you out of your money or wheedle you into marrying him.'

'O, your honour, I was never that sort o' woman, an' nobody has known it on me.'

'Very likely not, because you were never a widow before. A woman's always silly enough, but she's never quite as great a fool as she can be until she puts on a widow's cap. Now, just ask yourself how much the better you will be for staying on your farm at the end of four years, when you've got through your money, and let your farm run down, and are in arrears for half your rent; or, perhaps, have got some great hulky fellow for a husband, who swears at you and kicks your children.'

'Indeed, Sir Christifer, I know a deal o' farmin,' an' was brought up i' the thick on it, as you may say. An' there was my husband's great-aunt managed a farm for twenty year, an' left legacies to all her nephys an' nieces, an' even to my husband, as was then a babe unborn.'

'Psha! a woman six feet high, with a squint and sharp elbows, I daresay – a man in petticoats. Not a rosy-cheeked widow like you, Mrs Hartopp.'

'Indeed, your honour, I never heard of her squintin', an' they said as she might ha' been married o'er and o'er again, to people as had no call to hanker after her money.'

'Ay, ay, that's what you all think. Every man that looks at you wants to marry you, and would like you the better the more children you have and the less money. But it is useless to talk and cry. I have good reasons for my plans, and never alter them. What you have to do is to take the best of your stock, and to look out for some little place to go to, when you leave The Hollows. Now, go back to Mrs Bellamy's room, and ask her to give you a dish of tea.'

Mrs Hartopp, understanding from Sir Christopher's tone that he was not to be shaken, curtsied low and left the library, while the Baronet, seating himself at his desk in the oriel window, wrote the following letter:

*Mr Markham,*
*Take no steps about letting Crowsfoot Cottage, as I intend to put in the widow Hartopp when she leaves her farm, and if you will be here at eleven on Saturday morning, I will ride round with you, and settle about making some repairs, and see about adding a bit of land to the take, as she will want to keep a cow and some pigs.*
*Yours faithfully,*

*– Christopher Cheverel*

After ringing the bell and ordering this letter to be sent, Sir Christopher walked out to join the party on the lawn. But finding the cushions deserted, he walked on to the eastern front of the building, where, by the side of the grand entrance, was the large bow window of the saloon, opening on to the gravel sweep, and looking towards a long vista of undulating turf, bordered by tall trees, which, seeming to unite itself with the green of the meadows and a grassy road through a plantation, only terminated with the Gothic arch of a gateway in the far distance. The bow window was open, and Sir Christopher, stepping in, found the group he sought, examining the progress of the unfinished ceiling. It was in the same style of florid pointed Gothic as the dining room, but more elaborate in its tracery, which was like petrified lace-work picked out with delicate and varied colouring. About a fourth of it still remained uncoloured, and under this part were scaffolding, ladders, and tools; otherwise the spacious saloon was empty of furniture, and seemed to be a grand Gothic canopy for the group of five human figures standing in the centre.

'Francesco has been getting on a little better the last day or two,' said Sir Christopher, as he joined the party: 'he's a sad lazy dog, and I fancy he has a knack of sleeping as he stands, with his brushes in his hands. But I must spur him on, or we may not have the scaffolding cleared away before the bride comes, if you show dexterous generalship in your wooing, eh, Anthony? and take your Magdeburg[8] quickly.'

'Ah, sir, a siege is known to be one of the most tedious operations in war,' said Captain Wybrow, with an easy smile.

'Not when there's a traitor within the walls in the shape of a soft heart. And that there will be, if Beatrice has her mother's tenderness as well as her mother's beauty.'

'What do you think, Sir Christopher,' said Lady Cheverel, who seemed to wince a little under her husband's reminiscences, 'of hanging Guercino's[9] "Sibyl" over that door when we put up the pictures? It is rather lost in my sitting room.'

'Very good, my love,' answered Sir Christopher, in a tone of punctiliously polite affection; 'if you like to part with the ornament from your own room, it will show admirably here. Our portraits, by Sir Joshua, will hang opposite the window, and the "Transfiguration" at that end.

You see, Anthony, I am leaving no good places on the walls for you and your wife. We shall turn you with your faces to the wall in the gallery, and you may take your revenge on us by and by.'

While this conversation was going on, Mr Gilfil turned to Caterina and said, 'I like the view from this window better than any other in the house.'

She made no answer, and he saw that her eyes were filling with tears, so he added, 'Suppose we walk out a little; Sir Christopher and my lady seem to be occupied.'

Caterina complied silently, and they turned down one of the gravel walks that led, after many windings under tall trees and among grassy openings, to a large enclosed flower garden. Their walk was perfectly silent, for Maynard Gilfil knew that Caterina's thoughts were not with him, and she had been long used to make him endure the weight of those moods that she carefully hid from others. They reached the flower garden, and turned mechanically in at the gate that opened, through a high thick hedge, on an expanse of brilliant colour, which, after the green shades they had passed through, startled the eye like flames. The effect was assisted by an undulation of the ground, which gradually descended from the entrance gate, and then rose again towards the opposite end, crowned by an orangery. The flowers were glowing with their evening splendours; verbenas and heliotropes were sending up their finest incense. It seemed a gala where all was happiness and brilliancy, and misery could find no sympathy. This was the effect it had on Caterina. As she wound among the beds of gold and blue and pink, where the flowers seemed to be looking at her with wondering elf-like eyes, knowing nothing of sorrow, the feeling of isolation in her wretchedness overcame her, and the tears, which had been before trickling slowly down her pale cheeks, now gushed forth accompanied with sobs. And yet there was a loving human being close beside her, whose heart was aching for hers, who was possessed by the feeling that she was miserable, and that he was helpless to soothe her. But she was too much irritated by the idea that his wishes were different from hers, that he rather regretted the folly of her hopes than the probability of their disappointment, to take any comfort in his sympathy. Caterina, like the rest of us, turned away from sympathy that she suspected to be mingled with criticism, as the child turns away from the sweetmeat in which it suspects imperceptible medicine.

'Dear Caterina, I think I hear voices,' said Mr Gilfil; 'they may be coming this way.'

She checked herself like one accustomed to conceal her emotions, and ran rapidly to the other end of the garden, where she seemed occupied in selecting a rose. Presently Lady Cheverel entered, leaning on the arm of Captain Wybrow, and followed by Sir Christopher. The party stopped to admire the tiers of geraniums near the gate, and in the mean time Caterina tripped back with a moss rosebud in her hand, and, going up to Sir Christopher, said – 'There, Padroncello[10] – there is a nice rose for your buttonhole.'

'Ah, you black-eyed monkey,' he said, fondly stroking her cheek; 'so you have been running off with Maynard, either to torment or coax him an inch or two deeper into love. Come, come, I want you to sing us "*Ho perduto*"[11] before we sit down to picquet.[12] Anthony goes tomorrow, you know; you must warble him into the right sentimental lover's mood, that he may acquit himself well at Bath.' He put her little arm under his, and calling to Lady Cheverel, 'Come, Henrietta!' led the way towards the house.

The party entered the drawing room, which, with its oriel window, corresponded to the library in the other wing, and had also a flat ceiling heavy with carving and blazonry; but the window being unshaded, and the walls hung with full-length portraits of knights and dames in scarlet, white, and gold, it had not the sombre effect of the library. Here hung the portrait of Sir Anthony Cheverel, who in the reign of Charles II was the renovator of the family splendour, which had suffered some declension from the early brilliancy of that Chevreuil who came over with the Conqueror. A very imposing personage was this Sir Anthony, standing with one arm akimbo, and one fine leg and foot advanced, evidently with a view to the gratification of his contemporaries and posterity. You might have taken off his splendid peruke, and his scarlet cloak, which was thrown backward from his shoulders, without annihilating the dignity of his appearance. And he had known how to choose a wife, too, for his lady, hanging opposite to him, with her sunny brown hair drawn away in bands from her mild grave face, and falling in two large rich curls on her snowy gently sloping neck, which shamed the harsher hue and outline of her white satin robe, was a fit mother of 'large-acred' heirs.

In this room tea was served; and here, every evening, as regularly as the great clock in the courtyard with deliberate bass tones struck nine, Sir Christopher and Lady Cheverel sat down to picquet until half past ten, when Mr Gilfil read prayers to the assembled household in the chapel.

But now it was not near nine, and Caterina must sit down to the harpsichord and sing Sir Christopher's favourite airs, by Gluck and Paesiello, whose operas, for the happiness of that generation, were then to be heard on the London stage. It happened this evening that the sentiment of these airs, '*Che faro senza Eurydice?*'[13] and '*Ho perduto il bel sembiante*', in both of which the singer pours out his yearning after his lost love, came very close to Caterina's own feeling. But her emotion, instead of being a hindrance to her singing, gave her additional power. Her singing was what she could do best; it was her one point of superiority, in which it was probable she would excel the highborn beauty whom Anthony was to woo, and her love, her jealousy, her pride, her rebellion against her destiny, made one stream of passion that welled forth in the deep rich tones of her voice. She had a rare contralto, which Lady Cheverel, who had high musical taste, had been careful to preserve her from straining.

'Excellent, Catērina,' said Lady Cheverel, as there was a pause after the wonderful linked sweetness of '*Che faro*'. 'I never heard you sing that so well. Once more!'

It was repeated, and then came, '*Ho perduto*', which Sir Christopher encored, in spite of the clock, just striking nine. When the last note was dying out he said – 'There's a clever black-eyed monkey. Now bring out the table for picquet.'

Caterina drew out the table and placed the cards; then, with her rapid fairy suddenness of motion, threw herself on her knees, and clasped Sir Christopher's knee. He bent down, stroked her cheek and smiled.

'Caterina, that is foolish,' said Lady Cheverel. 'I wish you would leave off those stage-players' antics.'

She jumped up, arranged the music on the harpsichord, and then, seeing the Baronet and his lady seated at picquet, quietly glided out of the room.

Captain Wybrow had been leaning near the harpsichord during the singing, and the chaplain had thrown himself on a sofa at the end of the room. They both now took up a book. Mr Gilfil chose the last number of the *Gentleman's Magazine*; Captain Wybrow, stretched on an ottoman near the door, opened *Faublas*;[14] and there was perfect silence in the room that, ten minutes before, was vibrating to the passionate tones of Caterina.

She had made her way along the cloistered passages, now lighted here and there by a small oil lamp, to the grand staircase, which led directly to a gallery running along the whole eastern side of the building, where it was her habit to walk when she wished to be alone. The bright moonlight was streaming through the windows, throwing into strange light and shadow the heterogeneous objects that lined the long walls: Greek statues and busts of Roman emperors; low cabinets filled with curiosities, natural and antiquarian; tropical birds and huge horns of beasts; Hindoo gods and strange shells; swords and daggers, and bits of chain-armour; Roman lamps and tiny models of Greek temples; and, above all these, queer old family portraits – of little boys and girls, once the hope of the Cheverels, with close-shaven heads imprisoned in stiff ruffs – of faded, pink-faced ladies, with rudimentary features and highly developed headdresses – of gallant gentlemen, with high hips, high shoulders, and red pointed beards.

Here, on rainy days, Sir Christopher and his lady took their promenade, and here billiards were played, but, in the evening, it was forsaken by all except Caterina – and, sometimes, one other person.

She paced up and down in the moonlight, her pale face and thin white-robed form making her look like the ghost of some former Lady Cheverel come to revisit the glimpses of the moon.

By and by she paused opposite the broad window above the portico, and looked out on the long vista of turf and trees now stretching chill and saddened in the moonlight.

Suddenly a breath of warmth and roses seemed to float towards her, and an arm stole gently round her waist, while a soft hand took up her

27

tiny fingers. Caterina felt an electric thrill, and was motionless for one long moment; then she pushed away the arm and hand, and, turning round, lifted up to the face that hung over her eyes full of tenderness and reproach. The fawn-like unconsciousness was gone, and in that one look were the ground tones of poor little Caterina's nature – intense love and fierce jealousy.

'Why do you push me away, Tina?' said Captain Wybrow in a half-whisper; 'are you angry with me for what a hard fate puts upon me? Would you have me cross my uncle – who has done so much for us both – in his dearest wish? You know I have duties – we both have duties – before which feeling must be sacrificed.'

'Yes, yes,' said Caterina, stamping her foot, and turning away her head; 'don't tell me what I know already.'

There was a voice speaking in Caterina's mind to which she had never yet given vent. That voice said continually. 'Why did he make me love him – why did he let me know he loved me, if he knew all the while that he couldn't brave everything for my sake?' Then love answered, 'He was led on by the feeling of the moment, as you have been, Caterina; and now you ought to help him to do what is right.' Then the voice rejoined, 'It was a slight matter to him. He doesn't much mind giving you up. He will soon love that beautiful woman, and forget a poor little pale thing like you.'

Thus love, anger, and jealousy were struggling in that young soul.

'Besides, Tina,' continued Captain Wybrow in still gentler tones, 'I shall not succeed. Miss Assher very likely prefers someone else; and you know I have the best will in the world to fail. I shall come back a hapless bachelor – perhaps to find you already married to the good-looking chaplain, who is over head and ears in love with you. Poor Sir Christopher has made up his mind that you're to have Gilfil.'

'Why will you speak so? You speak from your own want of feeling. Go away from me.'

'Don't let us part in anger, Tina. All this may pass away. It's as likely as not that I may never marry anyone at all. These palpitations may carry me off, and you may have the satisfaction of knowing that I shall never be anybody's bridegroom. Who knows what may happen? I may be my own master before I get into the bonds of holy matrimony, and be able to choose my little singing-bird. Why should we distress ourselves before the time?'

'It is easy to talk so when you are not feeling,' said Caterina, the tears flowing fast. 'It is bad to bear now, whatever may come after. But you don't care about my misery.'

'Don't I, Tina?' said Anthony in his tenderest tones, again stealing his arm round her waist, and drawing her towards him. Poor Tina was the slave of this voice and touch. Grief and resentment, retrospect and foreboding, vanished – all life before and after melted away in the bliss of that moment, as Anthony pressed his lips to hers.

Captain Wybrow thought, 'Poor little Tina! it would make her very happy to have me. But she is a mad little thing.'

At that moment a loud bell startled Caterina from her trance of bliss. It was the summons to prayers in the chapel, and she hastened away, leaving Captain Wybrow to follow slowly.

It was a pretty sight, that family assembled to worship in the little chapel, where a couple of wax-candles threw a mild faint light on the figures kneeling there. In the desk was Mr Gilfil, with his face a shade graver than usual. On his right hand, kneeling on their red velvet cushions, were the master and mistress of the household, in their elderly dignified beauty. On his left, the youthful grace of Anthony and Caterina, in all the striking contrast of their colouring – he, with his exquisite outline and rounded fairness, like an Olympian god; she, dark and tiny, like a gypsy changeling. Then there were the domestics kneeling on red-covered forms, – the women headed by Mrs Bellamy, the natty little old housekeeper, in snowy cap and apron, and Mrs Sharp, my lady's maid, of somewhat vinegar aspect and flaunting attire; the men by Mr Bellamy the butler, and Mr Warren, Sir Christopher's venerable valet.

A few collects from the Evening Service was what Mr Gilfil habitually read, ending with the simple petition, 'Lighten our darkness.'

And then they all rose, the servants turning to curtsy and bow as they went out. The family returned to the drawing room, said goodnight to each other, and dispersed – all to speedy slumber except two. Caterina only cried herself to sleep after the clock had struck twelve. Mr Gilfil lay awake still longer, thinking that very likely Caterina was crying.

Captain Wybrow, having dismissed his valet at eleven, was soon in a soft slumber, his face looking like a fine cameo in high relief on the slightly indented pillow.

3

The last chapter has given the discerning reader sufficient insight into the state of things at Cheverel Manor in the summer of 1788. In that summer, we know, the great nation of France was agitated by conflicting thoughts and passions, which were but the beginning of sorrows. And in our Caterina's little breast, too, there were terrible struggles. The poor bird was beginning to flutter and vainly dash its soft breast against the hard iron bars of the inevitable, and we see too plainly the danger, if that anguish should go on heightening instead of being allayed, that the palpitating heart may be fatally bruised.

Meanwhile, if, as I hope, you feel some interest in Caterina and her friends at Cheverel Manor, you are perhaps asking, How came she to be there? How was it that this tiny, dark-eyed child of the south, whose face was immediately suggestive of olive-covered hills and taper-lit shrines, came to have her home in that stately English manor house, by the side of the blonde matron, Lady Cheverel – almost as if a humming-bird were found perched on one of the elm trees in the park, by the side of her ladyship's handsomest pouter-pigeon? Speaking good English, too, and joining in Protestant prayers! Surely she must have been adopted and brought over to England at a very early age. She was.

During Sir Christopher's last visit to Italy with his lady, fifteen years before, they resided for some time at Milan, where Sir Christopher, who was an enthusiast for Gothic architecture, and was then entertaining the project of metamorphosing his plain brick family mansion into the model of a Gothic manor house, was bent on studying the details of that marble miracle, the cathedral. Here Lady Cheverel, as at other Italian cities where she made any protracted stay, engaged a maestro to give her lessons in singing, for she had then not only fine musical taste, but a fine soprano voice. Those were days when very rich people used manuscript music, and many a man who resembled Jean Jacques in nothing else, resembled him in getting a livelihood '*à copier la musique à tant la page*'.[15] Lady Cheverel having need of this service, Maestro Albani told her he would send her a *poveraccio*[16] of his acquaintance, whose manuscript was the neatest and most correct he knew of. Unhappily, the *poveraccio* was not always in his best wits, and was sometimes rather slow in consequence, but it would be a work of Christian charity worthy of the beautiful Signora to employ poor Sarti.

The next morning, Mrs Sharp, then a blooming abigail[17] of three-and-thirty, entered her lady's private room and said, 'If you please, my lady, there's the frowsiest, shabbiest man you ever saw, outside, and he's told Mr Warren as the singing master sent him to see your ladyship. But I think you'll hardly like him to come in here. Belike he's only a beggar.'

'O yes, show him in immediately.'

Mrs Sharp retired, muttering something about 'fleas and worse'. She had the smallest possible admiration for fair Ausonia[18] and its natives, and even her profound deference for Sir Christopher and her lady could not prevent her from expressing her amazement at the infatuation of gentlefolks in choosing to sojourn among 'Papises, in countries where there was no getting to air a bit o' linen, and where the people smelt o' garlick fit to knock you down.'

However she presently reappeared, ushering in a small meagre man, sallow and dingy, with a restless wandering look in his dull eyes, and an excessive timidity about his deep reverences, which gave him the air of a man who had been long a solitary prisoner. Yet through all this squalor and wretchedness there were some traces discernible of comparative youth and former good looks. Lady Cheverel, though not very tender-hearted, still less sentimental, was essentially kind, and liked to dispense benefits like a goddess, who looks down benignly on the halt, the maimed, and the blind that approach her shrine. She was smitten with some compassion at the sight of poor Sarti, who struck her as the mere battered wreck of a vessel that might have once floated gaily enough on its outward voyage to the sound of pipes and tabors. She spoke gently as she pointed out to him the operatic selections she wished him to copy, and he seemed to sun himself in her auburn, radiant presence, so that when he made his exit with the music books under his arm, his bow, though not less reverent, was less timid.

It was ten years at least since Sarti had seen anything so bright and stately and beautiful as Lady Cheverel. For the time was far off in which he had trod the stage in satin and feathers, the *primo tenore*[19] of one short season. He had completely lost his voice in the following winter, and had ever since been little better than a cracked fiddle, which is good for nothing but firewood. For, like many Italian singers, he was too ignorant to teach, and if it had not been for his one talent of penmanship, he and his young helpless wife might have starved. Then, just after their third child was born, fever came, swept away the sickly mother and the two eldest children, and attacked Sarti himself, who rose from his sickbed with enfeebled brain and muscle, and a tiny baby on his hands, scarcely four months old. He lodged over a fruit shop kept by a stout virago, loud of tongue and irate in temper, but who had had children born to her, and so had taken care of the tiny yellow, black-eyed *bambinetto*,[20] and tended Sarti himself through his sickness. Here he continued to live, earning a meagre subsistence for himself and his little one by the work of copying music, put into his hands chiefly by Maestro Albani. He seemed to exist for nothing but the child: he tended it, he dandled it, he chatted to it, living with it alone in his one room above the fruit shop, only asking his landlady to take care of the marmoset during his short absences in fetching and carrying home work. Customers frequenting that fruit shop might often see the tiny Caterina seated on the floor with her legs in a heap of pease, which it was her delight to kick about; or perhaps deposited, like a kitten, in a large basket out of harm's way.

Sometimes, however, Sarti left his little one with another kind of protectress. He was very regular in his devotions, which he paid thrice a week in the great cathedral, carrying Caterina with him. Here, when the high morning sun was warming the myriad glittering pinnacles without, and struggling against the massive gloom within, the shadow of a man with a child on his arm might be seen flitting across the more stationary shadows of pillar and mullion, and making its way towards a little tinsel Madonna hanging in a retired spot near the choir. Amid all the sublimities of the mighty cathedral, poor Sarti had fixed on this tinsel Madonna as the symbol of divine mercy and protection, – just as a child, in the presence of a great landscape, sees none of the glories of wood and sky, but sets its heart on a floating feather or insect that happens to be on a level with its eye. Here, then, Sarti worshipped and prayed, setting Caterina on the floor by his side, and now and then, when the cathedral lay near some place where he had to call, and did not like to take her, he would leave her there in front of the tinsel Madonna, where she would sit, perfectly good, amusing herself with low crowing noises and see-sawings of her tiny body. And when Sarti came back, he always found that the Blessed Mother had taken good care of Caterina.

That was briefly the history of Sarti, who fulfilled so well the orders Lady Cheverel gave him, that she sent him away again with a stock of new work. But this time, week after week passed, and he neither reappeared nor sent home the music entrusted to him. Lady Cheverel began to be anxious, and was thinking of sending Warren to enquire at the address Sarti had given her, when one day, as she was equipped for driving out, the valet brought in a small piece of paper, which, he said, had been left for her ladyship by a man who was carrying fruit. The paper contained only three tremulous lines, in Italian: 'Will the Eccelentissima,[21] for the love of God, have pity on a dying man, and come to him?'

Lady Cheverel recognised the handwriting as Sarti's in spite of its tremulousness, and, going down to her carriage, ordered the Milanese coachman to drive to Strada Quinquagesima, Numero 10. The coach stopped in a dirty narrow street opposite La Pazzini's fruit shop, and that large specimen of womanhood immediately presented herself at the door, to the extreme disgust of Mrs Sharp, who remarked privately to Mr Warren that La Pazzini was a 'hijeous porpis'. The fruit-woman, however, was all smiles and deep curtsies to the Eccelentissima, who, not very well understanding her Milanese dialect, abbreviated the conversation by asking to be shown at once to Signor Sarti. La Pazzini preceded her up the dark narrow stairs, and opened a door through which she begged her ladyship to enter. Directly opposite the door lay Sarti, on a low miserable bed. His eyes were glazed, and no movement indicated that he was conscious of their entrance.

On the foot of the bed was seated a tiny child, apparently not three years old, her head covered by a linen cap, her feet clothed with leather boots, above which her little yellow legs showed thin and naked. A frock, made of what had once been a gay flowered silk, was her only other garment. Her large dark eyes shone from out her queer little face, like two precious stones in a grotesque image carved in old ivory. She held an empty medicine-bottle in her hand, and was amusing herself with putting the cork in and drawing it out again, to hear how it would pop.

La Pazzini went up to the bed and said, '*Ecco la nobilissima donna*,'[22] but directly after screamed out, 'Holy mother! he is dead!'

It was so. The entreaty had not been sent in time for Sarti to carry out his project of asking the great English lady to take care of his Caterina. That was the thought that haunted his feeble brain as soon as he began to fear that his illness would end in death. She had wealth – she was kind – she would surely do something for the poor orphan. And so, at last, he sent that scrap of paper that won the fulfilment of his prayer, though he did not live to utter it. Lady Cheverel gave La Pazzini money that the last decencies might be paid to the dead man, and carried away Caterina, meaning to consult Sir Christopher as to what should be done with her. Even Mrs Sharp had been so smitten with pity by the scene she had witnessed when she was summoned upstairs to fetch Caterina as to shed a small tear, though she was not at all subject to that weakness; indeed, she abstained from it on principle, because, as she often said, it was known to be the worst thing in the world for the eyes.

On the way back to her hotel, Lady Cheverel turned over various projects in her mind regarding Caterina, but at last one gained the preference over all the rest. Why should they not take the child to England, and bring her up there? They had been married twelve years, yet Cheverel Manor was cheered by no children's voices, and the old house would be all the better for a little of that music. Besides, it would be a Christian work to train this little Papist into a good Protestant, and graft as much English fruit as possible on the Italian stem.

Sir Christopher listened to this plan with hearty acquiescence. He loved children, and took at once to the little black-eyed monkey – his name for Caterina all through her short life. But neither he nor Lady Cheverel had any idea of adopting her as their daughter, and giving her

34

their own rank in life. They were much too English and aristocratic to think of anything so romantic. No! the child would be brought up at Cheverel Manor as a protégée, to be ultimately useful, perhaps, in sorting worsteds, keeping accounts, reading aloud, and otherwise supplying the place of spectacles when her ladyship's eyes should wax dim.

So Mrs Sharp had to procure new clothes, to replace the linen cap, flowered frock, and leathern boots, and now, strange to say, little Caterina, who had suffered many unconscious evils in her existence of thirty moons, first began to know conscious troubles. 'Ignorance,' says Ajax, 'is a painless evil;'[23] so, I should think, is dirt, considering the merry faces that go along with it. At any rate, cleanliness is sometimes a painful good, as anyone can vouch who has had his face washed the wrong way, by a pitiless hand with a gold ring on the third finger. If you, reader, have not known that initiatory anguish, it is idle to expect that you will form any approximate conception of what Caterina endured under Mrs Sharp's new dispensation of soap-and-water. Happily, this purgatory came presently to be associated in her tiny brain with a passage straightway to a seat of bliss – the sofa in Lady Cheverel's sitting room, where there were toys to be broken, a ride was to be had on Sir Christopher's knee, and a spaniel of resigned temper was prepared to undergo small tortures without flinching.

4

In three months from the time of Caterina's adoption – namely, in the late autumn of 1773 – the chimneys of Cheverel Manor were sending up unwonted smoke, and the servants were awaiting in excitement the return of their master and mistress after a two years' absence. Great was the astonishment of Mrs Bellamy, the housekeeper, when Mr Warren lifted a little black-eyed child out of the carriage, and great was Mrs Sharp's sense of superior information and experience, as she detailed Caterina's history, interspersed with copious comments, to the rest of the upper servants that evening, as they were taking a comfortable glass of grog together in the housekeeper's room.

A pleasant room it was as any party need desire to muster in on a cold November evening. The fireplace alone was a picture: a wide and deep recess with a low brick altar in the middle, where great logs of dry wood sent myriad sparks up the dark chimney throat, and over the front of this recess a large wooden entablature bearing this motto, finely carved in old English letters, 'Fear God and honour the King'. And beyond the party, who formed a half-moon with their chairs and well-furnished table round this bright fireplace, what a space of chiaroscuro for the imagination to revel in! Stretching across the far end of the room, what an oak table, high enough surely for Homer's gods, standing on four massive legs, bossed and bulging like sculptured urns! and, lining the distant wall, what vast cupboards, suggestive of inexhaustible apricot jam and promiscuous butler's perquisites! A stray picture or two had found their way down there, and made agreeable patches of dark brown on the buff-coloured walls. High over the loud-resounding double door hung one that, from some indications of a face looming out of blackness, might, by a great synthetic effort, be pronounced a Magdalen. Considerably lower down hung the similitude of a hat and feathers, with portions of a ruff, stated by Mrs Bellamy to represent Sir Francis Bacon,[24] who invented gunpowder, and, in her opinion, 'might ha' been better emplyed'.

But this evening the mind is but slightly arrested by the great Verulam, and is in the humour to think a dead philosopher less interesting than a living gardener, who sits conspicuous in the half-circle round the fireplace. Mr Bates is habitually a guest in the housekeeper's room of an evening, preferring the social pleasures there – the feast of gossip and the flow of grog – to a bachelor's chair in his charming thatched cottage on a little island, where every sound is remote, but the cawing of rooks and the screaming of wild geese, poetic sounds, doubtless, but, humanly speaking, not convivial.

Mr Bates was by no means an average person, to be passed without special notice. He was a sturdy Yorkshireman, approaching forty, whose face Nature seemed to have coloured when she was in a hurry, and had no time to attend to nuances, for every inch of him visible above his neckcloth was of one impartial redness, so that when he was at some distance your imagination was at liberty to place his lips anywhere between his nose and chin. Seen closer, his lips were discerned to be of a peculiar cut, and I fancy this had something to do with the peculiarity of his dialect, which, as we shall see, was individual rather than provincial. Mr Bates was further distinguished from the common herd by a perpetual blinking of the eyes; and this, together with the red-rose tint of his complexion, and a way he had of hanging his head forward, and rolling it from side to side as he walked, gave him the air of a Bacchus in a blue apron, who, in the present reduced circumstances of Olympus, had taken to the management of his own vines. Yet, as gluttons are often thin, so sober men are often rubicund, and Mr Bates was sober, with that manly, British, churchmanlike sobriety that can carry a few glasses of grog without any perceptible clarification of ideas.

'Dang my boottons!' observed Mr Bates, who, at the conclusion of Mrs Sharp's narrative, felt himself urged to his strongest interjection, 'it's what I shouldn't ha' looked for from Sir Cristhifer an' my ledy, to bring a furrin child into the coonthry; an' depend on't, whether you an' me lives to see't or noo, it'll coom to soom harm. The first sitiation iver I held – it was a hold hancient habbey, wi' the biggest orchard o' apples an' pears you ever see – there was a French valet, an' he stool silk stoockins, an' shirts, an' rings, an' iverythin' he could ley his hands on, an' run awey at last wi' th' missis's jewl-box. They're all alaike, them furriners. It roons i' th' blood.'

'Well,' said Mrs Sharp, with the air of a person who held liberal views, but knew where to draw the line, 'I'm not a-going to defend the furriners, for I've as good reason to know what they are as most folks, an' nobody'll ever hear me say but what they're next door to heathens, and the hile they eat wi' their victuals is enough to turn any Christian's stomach. But for all that – an' for all as the trouble in respect o' washin' and managin' has fell upo' me through the journey – I can't say but what I think as my Lady an' Sir Cristifer's done a right thing by a hinnicent child as doesn't know its right hand from its left, i' bringing it where it'll learn to speak summat better nor gibberish, and be brought up i' the true religion. For as for them furrin churches as Sir Cristifer is so unaccountable mad after, wi' pictures o' men an' women a-showing themselves just for all the world as God made 'em. I think, for my part, as it's welly a sin to go into 'em.'

'You're likely to have more foreigners, however,' said Mr Warren, who liked to provoke the gardener, 'for Sir Christopher has engaged some Italian workmen to help in the alterations in the house.'

'Olterations!' exclaimed Mrs Bellamy, in alarm. 'What olterations!'

'Why,' answered Mr Warren, 'Sir Christopher, as I understand, is going to make a new thing of the old manor house both inside and out. And he's got portfolios full of plans and pictures coming. It is to be cased with stone, in the Gothic style – pretty near like the churches, you know, as far as I can make out; and the ceilings are to be beyond anything that's been seen in the country. Sir Christopher's been giving a deal of study to it.'

'Dear heart alive!' said Mrs Bellamy, 'we shall be pisoned wi' lime an' plaster, an' hev the house full o' workmen colloguing wi' the maids, an' makin' no end o' mischief.'

'That ye may ley your life on, Mrs Bellamy,' said Mr Bates. 'Howiver, I'll noot denay that the Goothic stayle's prithy anoof, an' it's woonderful how near them stoon-carvers cuts oot the shapes o' the pine apples, an' shamrucks, an' rooses. I dare sey Sir Cristhifer'll meck a naice thing o' the Manor, an' there woon't be many gentlemen's houses i' the coonthry as'll coom up to't, wi' sich a garden an' pleasure-groons an' wall-fruit as King George maight be prood on.'

'Well, I can't think as the house can be better nor it is, Gothic or no Gothic,' said Mrs Bellamy; 'an' I've done the picklin' and preservin' in it fourteen year Michaelmas was a three weeks. But what does my lady say to't?'

'My lady knows better than cross Sir Cristifer in what he's set his mind on,' said Mr Bellamy, who objected to the critical tone of the conversation. 'Sir Cristifer'll hev his own way, *that* you may tek your oath. An' i' the right on't too. He's a gentleman born, an's got the money. But come, Mester Bates, fill your glass, an' we'll drink health an' happiness to his honour an' my lady, and then you shall give us a song. Sir Cristifer doesn't come hum from Italy ivery night.'

This demonstrable position was accepted without hesitation as ground for a toast, but Mr Bates, apparently thinking that his song was not an equally reasonable sequence, ignored the second part of Mr Bellamy's proposal. So Mrs Sharp, who had been heard to say that she had no thoughts at all of marrying Mr Bates, though he was 'a sensable fresh-coloured man as many a woman 'ud snap at for a husband', enforced Mr Bellamy's appeal.

'Come, Mr Bates, let us hear "Roy's Wife". I'd rether hear a good old song like that, nor all the fine Italian toodlin.'

Mr Bates, urged thus flatteringly, stuck his thumbs into the armholes of his waistcoat, threw himself back in his chair with his head in that position in which he could look directly towards the zenith, and struck up a remarkably staccato rendering of 'Roy's Wife of Aldivalloch'. This melody may certainly be taxed with excessive iteration, but that was precisely its highest recommendation to the present audience, who found it all the easier to swell the chorus. Nor did it at all diminish their pleasure that the only particular concerning 'Roy's Wife', which Mr Bates's enunciation allowed them to gather, was that she 'chated' him – whether in the matter of garden stuff or of some other commodity, or why her name should, in consequence, be repeatedly reiterated with exultation, remaining an agreeable mystery.

Mr Bates's song formed the climax of the evening's good-fellowship, and the party soon after dispersed – Mrs Bellamy perhaps to dream of quicklime flying among her preserving pans, or of lovesick housemaids reckless of unswept corners – and Mrs Sharp to sink into pleasant visions of independent housekeeping in Mr Bates's cottage, with no bells to answer, and with fruit and vegetables *ad libitum*.[25]

Caterina soon conquered all prejudices against her foreign blood, for what prejudices will hold out against helplessness and broken prattle? She became the pet of the household, thrusting Sir Christopher's favourite bloodhound of that day, Mrs Bellamy's two canaries, and Mr Bates's largest Dorking hen into a merely secondary position. The consequence was that in the space of a summer's day she went through a great cycle of experiences, commencing with the somewhat acid-ulated goodwill of Mrs Sharp's nursery discipline. Then came the grave luxury of her ladyship's sitting room, and, perhaps, the dignity of a ride on Sir Christopher's knee, sometimes followed by a visit with him to the stables, where Caterina soon learned to hear without crying the baying of the chained bloodhounds, and say, with ostentatious bravery, clinging to Sir Christopher's leg all the while, 'Dey not hurt Tina.'

Then Mrs Bellamy would perhaps be going out to gather the rose-leaves and lavender, and Tina was made proud and happy by being allowed to carry a handful in her pinafore; happier still, when they were spread out on sheets to dry, so that she could sit down like a frog among them, and have them poured over her in fragrant showers. Another frequent pleasure was to take a journey with Mr Bates through the kitchen gardens and the hothouses, where the rich bunches of green and purple grapes hung from the roof, far out of reach of the tiny yellow hand that could not help stretching itself out towards them; though the hand was sure at last to be satisfied with some delicate-flavoured fruit or sweet-scented flower. Indeed, in the long monotonous leisure of that great country house, you may be sure there was always someone who had nothing better to do than to play with Tina. So that the little southern bird had its northern nest lined with tenderness, and caresses, and pretty things. A loving sensitive nature was too likely, under such nurture, to have its susceptibility heightened into unfitness for an encounter with any harder experience, all the more, because there were gleams of fierce resistance to any discipline that had a harsh or unloving aspect. For the only thing in which Caterina showed any precocity was a certain ingenuity in vindictiveness. When she was five years old she had revenged herself for an unpleasant prohibition by pouring the ink into Mrs Sharp's work-basket, and once, when Lady Cheverel took her doll from her, because she was affectionately licking the paint off its face, the little minx straightway climbed on a chair and threw down a flower vase that stood on a bracket. This was almost the only instance in which her anger overcame her awe of Lady Cheverel, who had the ascendancy always belonging to kindness that never melts into caresses, and is severely but uniformly beneficent.

By and by the happy monotony of Cheverel Manor was broken in upon in the way Mr Warren had announced. The roads through the park were cut up by waggons carrying loads of stone from a neighbouring quarry, the green courtyard became dusty with lime, and the peaceful house rang with the sound of tools. For the next ten years Sir Christopher was occupied with the architectural metamorphosis of his old family mansion, thus anticipating, through the prompting of his individual taste, that general reaction from the insipid imitation of the

Palladian style towards a restoration of the Gothic, which marked the close of the eighteenth century. This was the object he had set his heart on, with a singleness of determination that was regarded with not a little contempt by his fox-hunting neighbours, who wondered greatly that a man with some of the best blood in England in his veins, should be mean enough to economise in his cellar, and reduce his stud to two old coach-horses and a hack, for the sake of riding a hobby, and playing the architect. Their wives did not see so much to blame in the matter of the cellar and stables, but they were eloquent in pity for poor Lady Cheverel, who had to live in no more than three rooms at once, and who must be distracted with noises, and have her constitution undermined by unhealthy smells. It was as bad as having a husband with an asthma. Why did not Sir Christopher take a house for her at Bath, or, at least, if he must spend his time in overlooking workmen, somewhere in the neighbourhood of the Manor? This pity was quite gratuitous, as the most plentiful pity always is, for though Lady Cheverel did not share her husband's architectural enthusiasm, she had too rigorous a view of a wife's duties, and too profound a deference for Sir Christopher, to regard submission as a grievance. As for Sir Christopher, he was perfectly indifferent to criticism. 'An obstinate, crotchety man,' said his neighbours. But I, who have seen Cheverel Manor, as he bequeathed it to his heirs, rather attribute that unswerving architectural purpose of his, conceived and carried out through long years of systematic personal exertion, to something of the fervour of genius, as well as inflexibility of will, and in walking through those rooms, with their splendid ceilings and their meagre furniture, which tell how all the spare money had been absorbed before personal comfort was thought of, I have felt that there dwelt in this old English baronet some of that sublime spirit that distinguishes art from luxury, and worships beauty apart from self-indulgence.

While Cheverel Manor was growing from ugliness into beauty, Caterina too was growing from a little yellow bantling into a whiter maiden, with no positive beauty indeed, but with a certain light airy grace, which, with her large appealing dark eyes, and a voice that, in its low-toned tenderness, recalled the love-notes of the stock dove, gave her a more than usual charm. Unlike the building, however, Caterina's development was the result of no systematic or careful appliances. She grew up very much like the primroses, which the gardener is not sorry to see within his enclosure, but takes no pains to cultivate. Lady Cheverel taught her to read and write, and say her catechism; Mr Warren, being a good accountant, gave her lessons in arithmetic, by her ladyship's desire; and Mrs Sharp initiated her in all the mysteries of the needle. But, for a long time, there was no thought of giving her any more elaborate education. It is very likely that to her dying day Caterina thought the earth stood still, and that the sun and stars moved round it, but so, for the matter of that, did Helen, and Dido, and Desdemona, and Juliet; whence I hope you will not think my Caterina less worthy to be a heroine on that account. The truth is, that, with one exception, her only talent lay in loving, and there, it is probable, the most astronomical of women could not have surpassed her. Orphan and protégée though she was, this supreme talent of hers found plenty of exercise at Cheverel Manor, and Caterina had more people to love than many a small lady and gentleman affluent in silver mugs and blood relations. I think the first place in her childish heart was given to Sir Christopher, for little girls are apt to attach themselves to the finest-looking gentleman at hand, especially as he seldom has anything to do with discipline. Next to the Baronet came Dorcas, the merry rosy-cheeked damsel who was Mrs Sharp's lieutenant in the nursery, and thus played the part of the raisins in a dose of senna. It was a black day for Caterina when Dorcas married the coachman, and went, with a great sense of elevation in the world, to preside over a 'public' in the noisy town of Sloppeter. A little china box, bearing the motto 'Though lost to sight, to memory dear', which Dorcas sent her as a remembrance, was among Caterina's treasures ten years after.

The one other exceptional talent, you already guess, was music. When the fact that Caterina had a remarkable ear for music, and a still more remarkable voice, attracted Lady Cheverel's notice, the discovery was very welcome both to her and Sir Christopher. Her musical education became at once an object of interest. Lady Cheverel devoted much time to it, and the rapidity of Tina's progress surpassing all hopes, an Italian singing master was engaged, for several years, to spend some months together at Cheverel Manor. This unexpected gift made a great alteration in Caterina's position. After those first years in which little girls are petted like puppies and kittens, there comes a time when it seems less obvious what they can be good for, especially when, like Caterina, they give no particular promise of cleverness or beauty, and it is not surprising that in that uninteresting period there was no particular plan formed as to her future position. She could always help Mrs Sharp, supposing she were fit for nothing else, as she grew up, but now, this rare gift of song endeared her to Lady Cheverel, who loved music above all things, and it associated her at once with the pleasures of the drawing room. Insensibly she came to be regarded as one of the family, and the servants began to understand that Miss Sarti was to be a lady after all.

'And the raight on't too,' said Mr Bates, 'for she hasn't the cut of a gell as must work for her bread; she's as nesh an' dilicate as a paich-blossom – welly laike a linnet, wi' on'y joost body anoof to hold her voice.'

But long before Tina had reached this stage of her history, a new era had begun for her, in the arrival of a younger companion than any she had hitherto known. When she was no more than seven, a ward of Sir Christopher's – a lad of fifteen, Maynard Gilfil by name – began to spend his vacations at Cheverel Manor, and found there no playfellow so much to his mind as Caterina. Maynard was an affectionate lad, who retained a propensity to white rabbits, pet squirrels, and guinea pigs, perhaps a little beyond the age at which young gentlemen usually look down on such pleasures as puerile. He was also much given to fishing, and to carpentry, considered as a fine art, without any base view to utility. And in all these pleasures it was his delight to have Caterina as his companion, to call her little pet names, answer her wondering questions, and have her toddling after him as you may have seen a Blenheim spaniel trotting after a large setter. Whenever Maynard went back to school, there was a little scene of parting.

'You won't forget me, Tina, before I come back again? I shall leave you all the whip-cord we've made; and don't you let Guinea die. Come, give me a kiss, and promise not to forget me.'

As the years wore on, and Maynard passed from school to college, and from a slim lad to a stalwart young man, their companionship in the vacations necessarily took a different form, but it retained a brotherly and sisterly familiarity. With Maynard the boyish affection had insensibly grown into ardent love. Among all the many kinds of first love, that which begins in childish companionship is the strongest and most enduring: when passion comes to unite its force to long affection, love is at its spring tide. And Maynard Gilfil's love was of a kind to make him prefer being tormented by Caterina to any pleasure, apart from her, which the most benevolent magician could have devised for him. It is the way with those tall large-limbed men, from Samson downwards. As for Tina, the little minx was perfectly well aware that Maynard was her slave; he was the one person in the world whom she did as she pleased with, and I need not tell you that this was a symptom of her being perfectly heart-whole so far as he was concerned: for a passionate woman's love is always overshadowed by fear.

Maynard Gilfil did not deceive himself in his interpretation of Caterina's feelings, but he nursed the hope that some time or other she would at least care enough for him to accept his love. So he waited patiently for the day when he might venture to say, 'Caterina, I love you!' You see, he would have been content with very little, being one of those men who pass through life without making the least clamour about themselves, thinking neither the cut of his coat, nor the flavour of his soup, nor the precise depth of a servant's bow, at all momentous. He thought – foolishly enough, as lovers *will* think – that it was a good augury for him when he came to be domesticated at Cheverel Manor in the quality of chaplain there, and curate of a neighbouring parish; judging falsely, from his own case, that habit and affection were the likeliest avenues to love. Sir Christopher satisfied several feelings in installing Maynard as chaplain in his house. He liked the old-fashioned dignity of that domestic appendage; he liked his ward's companionship; and, as Maynard had some private fortune, he might take life easily in that agreeable home, keeping his hunter, and observing a mild regimen of clerical duty, until the Cumbermoor living should fall in, when he might be settled for life in the neighbourhood of the manor. 'With Caterina for a wife, too,' Sir Christopher soon began to think, for though the good Baronet was not at all quick to suspect what was unpleasant and opposed to his views of fitness, he was quick to see what would dovetail with his own plans, and he had first guessed, and then ascertained, by direct enquiry, the state of Maynard's feelings. He at once leaped to the conclusion that Caterina was of the same mind, or at least would be, when she was old enough. But these were too early days for anything definite to be said or done.

Meanwhile, new circumstances were arising, which, though they made no change in Sir Christopher's plans and prospects, converted Mr Gilfil's hopes into anxieties, and made it clear to him not only that Caterina's heart was never likely to be his, but that it was given entirely to another.

Once or twice in Caterina's childhood, there had been another boy-visitor at the manor, younger than Maynard Gilfil – a beautiful boy with brown curls and splendid clothes, on whom Caterina had looked with shy admiration. This was Anthony Wybrow, the son of Sir Christopher's youngest sister, and chosen heir of Cheverel Manor. The Baronet had sacrificed a large sum, and even straitened the resources by which he was to carry out his architectural schemes, for the sake of removing the entail from his estate, and making this boy his heir – moved to the step, I am sorry to say, by an implacable quarrel with his elder sister, for a power of forgiveness was not among Sir Christopher's virtues. At length, on the death of Anthony's mother, when he was no longer a curly-headed boy, but a tall young man, with a captain's commission, Cheverel Manor became *his* home too, whenever he was absent from his regiment. Caterina was then a little woman, between sixteen and seventeen, and I need not spend many words in explaining what you perceive to be the most natural thing in the world.

There was little company kept at the Manor, and Captain Wybrow would have been much duller if Caterina had not been there. It was pleasant to pay her attentions – to speak to her in gentle tones, to see her little flutter of pleasure, the blush that just lit up her pale cheek, and the momentary timid glance of her dark eyes, when he praised her singing, leaning at her side over the piano. Pleasant, too, to cut out that chaplain with his large calves! What idle man can withstand the temptation of a woman to fascinate, and another man to eclipse? – especially when it is quite clear to himself that he means no mischief, and shall leave everything to come right again by and by? At the end of eighteen months, however, during which Captain Wybrow had spent much of his time at the Manor, he found that matters had reached a point that he had not at all contemplated. Gentle tones had led to tender words, and tender words had called forth a response of looks that made it impossible not to carry on the crescendo of love-making. To find one's self adored by a little, graceful, dark-eyed, sweet-singing woman, whom no one need despise, is an agreeable sensation, comparable to smoking the finest Latakia,[26] and also imposes some return of tenderness as a duty.

Perhaps you think that Captain Wybrow, who knew that it would be ridiculous to dream of his marrying Caterina, must have been a reckless libertine to win her affections in this manner! Not at all. He was a young man of calm passions, who was rarely led into any conduct of which he could not give a plausible account to himself, and the tiny fragile Caterina was a woman who touched the imagination and the affections rather than the senses. He really felt very kindly towards her, and would very likely have loved her – if he had been able to love anyone. But nature had not endowed him with that capability. She had given him an admirable figure, the whitest of hands, the most delicate of nostrils, and a large amount of serene self-satisfaction, but, as if to save such a delicate piece of work from any risk of being shattered, she had guarded him from the liability to a strong emotion. There was no list of youthful misdemeanours on record against him, and Sir Christopher and Lady Cheverel thought him the best of nephews, the most satisfactory of heirs, full of grateful deference to themselves, and, above all things, guided by a sense of duty. Captain Wybrow always did the thing easiest and most agreeable to him from a sense of duty: he dressed expensively, because it was a duty he owed to his position; from a sense of duty he adapted himself to Sir Christopher's inflexible will, which it would have been troublesome as well as useless to resist; and, being of a delicate constitution, he took care of his health from a sense of duty. His health was the only point on which he gave anxiety to his friends, and it was owing to this that Sir Christopher wished to see his nephew early married, the more so as a match after the Baronet's own heart appeared immediately attainable. Anthony had seen and admired Miss Assher, the only child of a lady who had been Sir Christopher's earliest love, but who, as things will happen in this world, had married another baronet instead of him. Miss Assher's father was now dead, and she was in possession of a pretty estate. If, as was probable, she should prove susceptible to the merits of Anthony's person and character, nothing could make Sir Christopher so happy as to see a marriage that might be expected to secure the inheritance of Cheverel Manor from getting into the wrong hands. Anthony had already been kindly received by Lady Assher as the nephew of her early friend; why should he not go to Bath, where she and her daughter were then residing, follow up the acquaintance, and win a handsome, well-born, and sufficiently wealthy bride?

Sir Christopher's wishes were communicated to his nephew, who at once intimated his willingness to comply with them – from a sense of duty. Caterina was tenderly informed by her lover of the sacrifice demanded from them both, and three days afterwards occurred the parting scene you have witnessed in the gallery, on the eve of Captain Wybrow's departure for Bath.

## 5

The inexorable ticking of the clock is like the throb of pain to sensations made keen by a sickening fear. And so it is with the great clockwork of nature. Daisies and buttercups give way to the brown waving grasses, tinged with the warm red sorrel; the waving grasses are swept away, and the meadows lie like emeralds set in the bushy hedgerows; the tawny-tipped corn begins to bow with the weight of the full ear; the reapers are bending amongst it, and it soon stands in sheaves, then presently, the patches of yellow stubble lie side by side with streaks of dark-red earth, which the plough is turning up in preparation for the new-thrashed seed. And this passage from beauty to beauty, which to the happy is like the flow of a melody, measures for many a human heart the approach of foreseen anguish – seems hurrying on the moment when the shadow of dread will be followed up by the reality of despair.

How cruelly hasty that summer of 1788 seemed to Caterina! Surely the roses vanished earlier, and the berries on the mountain ash were more impatient to redden, and bring on the autumn, when she would be face to face with her misery, and witness Anthony giving all his gentle tones, tender words, and soft looks to another.

Before the end of July, Captain Wybrow had written word that Lady Assher and her daughter were about to fly from the heat and gaiety of Bath to the shady quiet of their place at Farleigh, and that he was invited to join the party there. His letters implied that he was on an excellent footing with both the ladies, and gave no hint of a rival, so that Sir Christopher was more than usually bright and cheerful after reading them. At length, towards the close of August, came the announcement that Captain Wybrow was an accepted lover, and after much complimentary and congratulatory correspondence between the two families, it was understood that in September Lady Assher and her daughter would pay a visit to Cheverel Manor, when Beatrice would make the acquaintance of her future relatives, and all needful arrangements could be discussed. Captain Wybrow would remain at Farleigh till then, and accompany the ladies on their journey.

In the interval, everyone at Cheverel Manor had something to do by way of preparing for the visitors. Sir Christopher was occupied in consultations with his steward and lawyer, and in giving orders to everyone else, especially in spurring on Francesco to finish the saloon. Mr Gilfil had the responsibility of procuring a lady's horse, Miss Assher being a great rider. Lady Cheverel had unwonted calls to make and invitations to deliver. Mr Bates's turf, and gravel, and flower beds were always at such a point of neatness and finish that nothing extraordinary could be done in the garden, except a little extraordinary scolding of the under-gardener, and this addition Mr Bates did not neglect.

Happily for Caterina, she too had her task, to fill up the long dreary daytime: it was to finish a chair-cushion that would complete the set of embroidered covers for the drawing room, Lady Cheverel's year-long work, and the only noteworthy bit of furniture in the Manor. Over this embroidery she sat with cold lips and a palpitating heart, thankful that this miserable sensation throughout the daytime seemed to counteract the tendency to tears that returned with night and solitude. She was most frightened when Sir Christopher approached her. The Baronet's eye was brighter and his step more elastic than ever, and it seemed to him that only the most leaden or churlish souls could be otherwise than brisk and exulting in a world where everything went so well. Dear old gentleman! he had gone through life a little flushed with the power of his will, and now his latest plan was succeeding, and Cheverel Manor would be inherited by a grand-nephew, whom he might even yet live to see a fine young fellow with at least the down on his chin. Why not? one is still young at sixty.

Sir Christopher had always something playful to say to Caterina.

'Now, little monkey, you must be in your best voice: you're the minstrel of the Manor, you know, and be sure you have a pretty gown and a new ribbon. You must not be dressed in russet, though you are a singing-bird.' Or perhaps, 'It is your turn to be courted next, Tina. But don't you learn any naughty proud airs. I must have Maynard let off easily.'

Caterina's affection for the old Baronet helped her to summon up a smile as he stroked her cheek and looked at her kindly, but that was the moment at which she felt it most difficult not to burst out crying. Lady Cheverel's conversation and presence were less trying, for her ladyship felt no more than calm satisfaction in this family event, and besides, she was further sobered by a little jealousy at Sir Christopher's anticipation of pleasure in seeing Lady Assher, enshrined in his memory as a mild-eyed beauty of sixteen, with whom he had exchanged locks before he went on his first travels. Lady Cheverel would have died rather than confess it, but she couldn't help hoping that he would be disappointed in Lady Assher, and rather ashamed of having called her so charming.

Mr Gilfil watched Caterina through these days with mixed feelings. Her suffering went to his heart; but, even for her sake, he was glad that a love that could never come to good should be no longer fed by false hopes; and how could he help saying to himself, 'Perhaps, after a while, Caterina will be tired of fretting about that cold-hearted puppy, and then…'

At length the much-expected day arrived, and the brightest of September suns was lighting up the yellowing lime trees, as about five o'clock Lady Assher's carriage drove under the portico. Caterina, seated at work in her own room, heard the rolling of the wheels, followed presently by the opening and shutting of doors, and the sound of voices in the corridors. Remembering that the dinner-hour was six, and that Lady Cheverel had desired her to be in the drawing room early, she started up to dress, and was delighted to find herself feeling suddenly brave and strong. Curiosity to see Miss Assher – the thought that Anthony was in the house – the wish not to look unattractive, were feelings that brought some colour to her lips, and made it easy to attend to her toilette. They would ask her to sing this evening, and she would sing well. Miss Assher should not think her utterly insignificant. So she put on her grey silk gown and her cherry-coloured ribbon with as much care as if she had been herself the betrothed, not forgetting the pair of round pearl earrings that Sir Christopher had told Lady Cheverel to give her, because Tina's little ears were so pretty.

Quick as she had been, she found Sir Christopher and Lady Cheverel in the drawing room chatting with Mr Gilfil, and telling him how handsome Miss Assher was, but how entirely unlike her mother – apparently resembling her father only.

'Aha!' said Sir Christopher, as he turned to look at Caterina, 'what do you think of this, Maynard? Did you ever see Tina look so pretty before? Why, that little grey gown has been made out of a bit of my lady's, hasn't it? It doesn't take anything much larger than a pocket handkerchief to dress the little monkey.'

Lady Cheverel, too, serenely radiant in the assurance a single glance had given her of Lady Assher's inferiority, smiled approval, and Caterina was in one of those moods of self possession and indifference that come as the ebb tide between the struggles of passion. She retired to the piano, and busied herself with arranging her music, not at all insensible to the pleasure of being looked at with admiration the while, and thinking that, the next time the door opened, Captain Wybrow would enter, and she would speak to him quite cheerfully. But when she heard him come in, and the scent of roses floated towards her, her heart gave one great leap. She knew nothing till he was pressing her hand, and saying, in the old easy way, 'Well, Caterina, how do you do? You look quite blooming.'

She felt her cheeks reddening with anger that he could speak and look with such perfect nonchalance. Ah! he was too deeply in love with someone else to remember anything he had felt for *her*. But the next moment she was conscious of her folly – 'as if he could show any feeling then!' This conflict of emotions stretched into a long interval the few moments that elapsed before the door opened again, and her own attention, as well as that of all the rest, was absorbed by the entrance of the two ladies.

The daughter was the more striking, from the contrast she presented to her mother, a round-shouldered, middle-sized woman, who had once had the transient pink-and-white beauty of a blonde, with ill-defined features and early embonpoint. Miss Assher was tall, and gracefully though substantially formed, carrying herself with an air of mingled graciousness and self-confidence; her dark brown hair, untouched by powder, hanging in bushy curls round her face, and falling in long thick ringlets nearly to her waist. The brilliant carmine tint of her well-rounded cheeks, and the finely cut outline of her straight nose, produced an impression of splendid beauty, in spite of commonplace brown eyes, a narrow forehead, and thin lips. She was in mourning, and the dead black of her crape dress, relieved here and there by jet ornaments, gave the fullest effect to her complexion, and to the rounded whiteness of her arms, bare from the elbow. The first *coup d'oeil*[27] was dazzling, and as she stood looking down with a gracious smile on Caterina, whom Lady Cheverel was presenting to her, the poor little thing seemed to herself to feel, for the first time, all the folly of her former dream.

'We are enchanted with your place, Sir Christopher,' said Lady Assher, with a feeble kind of pompousness, which she seemed to be copying from someone else: 'I'm sure your nephew must have thought Farleigh wretchedly out of order. Poor Sir John was so very careless about keeping up the house and grounds. I often talked to him about it, but he said, "Pooh pooh! as long as my friends find a good dinner and a good bottle of wine, they won't care about my ceilings being rather smoky." He was so very hospitable, was Sir John.'

'I think the view of the house from the park, just after we passed the bridge, particularly fine,' said Miss Assher, interposing rather eagerly, as if she feared her mother might be making infelicitous speeches, 'and the pleasure of the first glimpse was all the greater because Anthony would describe nothing to us beforehand. He would not spoil our first impressions by raising false ideas. I long to go over the house, Sir Christopher, and learn the history of all your architectural designs, which Anthony says have cost you so much time and study.'

'Take care how you set an old man talking about the past, my dear,' said the Baronet; 'I hope we shall find something pleasanter for you to do than turning over my old plans and pictures. Our friend Mr Gilfil here has found a beautiful mare for you and you can scour the country to your heart's content. Anthony has sent us word what a horsewoman you are.'

Miss Assher turned to Mr Gilfil with her most beaming smile, and expressed her thanks with the elaborate graciousness of a person who means to be thought charming, and is sure of success.

'Pray do not thank me,' said Mr Gilfil, 'till you have tried the mare. She has been ridden by Lady Sara Linter for the last two years, but one lady's taste may not be like another's in horses, any more than in other matters.'

While this conversation was passing, Captain Wybrow was leaning against the mantelpiece, contenting himself with responding from under his indolent eyelids to the glances Miss Assher was constantly directing towards him as she spoke. 'She is very much in love with him,' thought Caterina. But she was relieved that Anthony remained passive in his attentions. She thought, too, that he was looking paler and more languid than usual. 'If he didn't love her very much – if he sometimes thought of the past with regret, I think I could bear it all, and be glad to see Sir Christopher made happy.'

During dinner there was a little incident that confirmed these thoughts. When the sweets were on the table, there was a mould of jelly just opposite Captain Wybrow, and being inclined to take some himself, he first invited Miss Assher, who coloured and said, in rather a sharper key than usual, 'Have you not learned by this time that I never take jelly?'

'Don't you?' said Captain Wybrow, whose perceptions were not acute enough for him to notice the difference of a semitone. 'I should have thought you were fond of it. There was always some on the table at Farleigh, I think.'

'You don't seem to take much interest in my likes and dislikes.'

'I'm too much possessed by the happy thought that you like me,' was the ex officio[28] reply, in silvery tones.

This little episode was unnoticed by everyone but Caterina. Sir Christopher was listening with polite attention to Lady Assher's history of her last man-cook, who was first-rate at gravies, and for that reason pleased Sir John – he was so particular about his gravies, was Sir John: and so they kept the man six years in spite of his bad pastry. Lady Cheverel and Mr Gilfil were smiling at Rupert the bloodhound, who had pushed his great head under his master's arm, and was taking a survey of the dishes, after snuffing at the contents of the Baronet's plate.

When the ladies were in the drawing room again, Lady Assher was soon deep in a statement to Lady Cheverel of her views about burying people in woollen.

'To be sure, you must have a woollen dress, because it's the law,[29] you know; but that need hinder no one from putting linen underneath. I always used to say, "If Sir John died tomorrow, I would bury him in his shirt;" and I did. And let me advise you to do so by Sir Christopher. You never saw Sir John, Lady Cheverel. He was a large tall man, with a nose just like Beatrice, and so very particular about his shirts.'

Miss Assher, meanwhile, had seated herself by Caterina, and, with that smiling affability that seems to say, 'I am really not at all proud, though you might expect it of me,' said, 'Anthony tells me you sing so very beautifully. I hope we shall hear you this evening.'

'O yes,' said Caterina, quietly, without smiling; 'I always sing when I am wanted to sing.'

'I envy you such a charming talent. Do you know, I have no ear; I cannot hum the smallest tune, and I delight in music so. Is it not unfortunate? But I shall have quite a treat while I am here; Captain Wybrow says you will give us some music every day.'

'I should have thought you wouldn't care about music if you had no ear,' said Caterina, becoming epigrammatic by force of grave simplicity.

'O, I assure you, I dote on it; and Anthony is so fond of it; it would be so delightful if I could play and sing to him, though he says he likes me best not to sing, because it doesn't belong to his idea of me. What style of music do you like best?'

'I don't know. I like all beautiful music.'

'And are you as fond of riding as of music?'

'No; I never ride. I think I should be very frightened.'

'O no! indeed you would not, after a little practice. I have never been in the least timid. I think Anthony is more afraid for me than I am for myself, and since I have been riding with him, I have been obliged to be more careful, because he is so nervous about me.'

Caterina made no reply, but she said to herself, 'I wish she would go away and not talk to me. She only wants me to admire her good nature, and to talk about Anthony.'

Miss Assher was thinking at the same time, 'This Miss Sarti seems a stupid little thing. Those musical people often are. But she is prettier than I expected; Anthony said she was not pretty.'

Happily at this moment Lady Assher called her daughter's attention to the embroidered cushions, and Miss Assher, walking to the opposite sofa, was soon in conversation with Lady Cheverel about tapestry and embroidery in general, while her mother, feeling herself superseded there, came and placed herself beside Caterina.

'I hear you are the most beautiful singer,' was of course the opening remark. 'All Italians sing so beautifully. I travelled in Italy with Sir John when we were first married, and we went to Venice, where they go about in gondolas, you know. You don't wear powder, I see. No more will Beatrice, though many people think her curls would look all the better for powder. She has so much hair, hasn't she? Our last maid dressed it much better than this, but, do you know, she wore Beatrice's stockings before they went to the wash, and we couldn't keep her after that, could we?'

Caterina, accepting the question as a mere bit of rhetorical effect, thought it superfluous to reply, till Lady Assher repeated, 'Could we, now?' as if Tina's sanction were essential to her repose of mind. After a faint 'No', she went on.

'Maids are so very troublesome, and Beatrice is so particular, you can't imagine. I often say to her, "My dear, you can't have perfection." That very gown she has on – to be sure, it fits her beautifully now – but it has been unmade and made up again twice. But she is like poor Sir John – he was so very particular about his own things, was Sir John. Is Lady Cheverel particular?'

'Rather. But Mrs Sharp has been her maid twenty years.'

'I wish there was any chance of our keeping Griffin twenty years. But I am afraid we shall have to part with her because her health is so delicate, and she is so obstinate, she will not take bitters as I want her. *You* look delicate, now. Let me recommend you to take camomile tea in a morning, fasting. Beatrice is so strong and healthy, she never takes any medicine, but if I had had twenty girls, and they had been delicate, I should have given them all camomile tea. It strengthens the constitution beyond anything. Now, will you promise me to take camomile tea?'

'Thank you: I'm not at all ill,' said Caterina. 'I've always been pale and thin.'

Lady Assher was sure camomile tea would make all the difference in the world – Caterina must see if it wouldn't – and then went dribbling on like a leaky shower-bath, until the early entrance of the gentlemen created a diversion, and she fastened on Sir Christopher, who probably began to think that, for poetical purposes, it would be better not to meet one's first love again, after a lapse of forty years.

Captain Wybrow, of course, joined his aunt and Miss Assher, and Mr Gilfil tried to relieve Caterina from the awkwardness of sitting aloof and dumb, by telling her how a friend of his had broken his arm and staked his horse that morning, not at all appearing to heed that she hardly listened, and was looking towards the other side of the room. One of the tortures of jealousy is that it can never turn its eyes away from the thing that pains it.

By and by everyone felt the need of a relief from chit-chat – Sir Christopher perhaps the most of all – and it was he who made the acceptable proposition –

'Come, Tina, are we to have no music tonight before we sit down to cards? Your ladyship plays at cards, I think?' he added, recollecting himself, and turning to Lady Assher.

'O yes! Poor dear Sir John would have a whist-table every night.'

Caterina sat down to the harpsichord at once, and had no sooner begun to sing than she perceived with delight that Captain Wybrow was gliding towards the harpsichord, and soon standing in the old place. This consciousness gave fresh strength to her voice, and when she noticed that Miss Assher presently followed him with that air of ostentatious admiration that belongs to the absence of real enjoyment, her closing bravura was none the worse for being animated by a little triumphant contempt.

'Why, you are in better voice than ever, Caterina,' said Captain Wybrow, when she had ended. 'This is rather different from Miss Hibbert's small piping that we used to be glad of at Farleigh, is it not, Beatrice?'

'Indeed it is. You are a most enviable creature, Miss Sarti – Caterina – may I not call you Caterina? for I have heard Anthony speak of you so often, I seem to know you quite well. You will let me call you Caterina?'

'O yes, everyone calls me Caterina, only when they call me Tina.'

'Come, come, more singing, more singing, little monkey,' Sir Christopher called out from the other side of the room. 'We have not had half enough yet.'

Caterina was ready enough to obey, for while she was singing she was queen of the room, and Miss Assher was reduced to grimacing admiration. Alas! you see what jealousy was doing in this poor young soul. Caterina, who had passed her life as a little unobtrusive singing-bird, nestling so fondly under the wings that were outstretched for her, her heart beating only to the peaceful rhythm of love, or fluttering with some easily stifled fear, had begun to know the fierce palpitations of triumph and hatred.

When the singing was over, Sir Christopher and Lady Cheverel sat down to whist with Lady Assher and Mr Gilfil, and Caterina placed herself at the Baronet's elbow, as if to watch the game, that she might not appear to thrust herself on the pair of lovers. At first she was glowing with her little triumph, and felt the strength of pride, but her eye *would* steal to the opposite side of the fireplace, where Captain Wybrow had seated himself close to Miss Assher, and was leaning with his arm over the back of the chair, in the most lover-like position. Caterina began to feel a choking sensation. She could see, almost without looking, that he was taking up her arm to examine her bracelet; their heads were bending close together, her curls touching his cheek – now he was putting his lips to her hand. Caterina felt her cheeks burn – she could sit no longer. She got up, pretended to be gliding about in search of something, and at length slipped out of the room.

Outside, she took a candle, and, hurrying along the passages and up the stairs to her own room, locked the door.

'O, I cannot bear it, I cannot bear it!' the poor thing burst out aloud, clasping her little fingers, and pressing them back against her forehead, as if she wanted to break them.

Then she walked hurriedly up and down the room.

'And this must go on for days and days, and I must see it.'

She looked about nervously for something to clutch. There was a muslin kerchief lying on the table; she took it up and tore it into shreds as she walked up and down, and then pressed it into hard balls in her hand.

'And Anthony,' she thought, 'he can do this without caring for what I feel. O, he can forget everything: how he used to say he loved me – how he used to take my hand in his as we walked – how he used to stand near me in the evenings for the sake of looking into my eyes.'

'Oh, it is cruel, it is cruel!' she burst out again aloud, as all those love-moments in the past returned upon her. Then the tears gushed forth, she threw herself on her knees by the bed, and sobbed bitterly.

She did not know how long she had been there, till she was startled by the prayer-bell; when, thinking Lady Cheverel might perhaps send someone to enquire after her, she rose, and began hastily to undress, that there might be no possibility of her going down again. She had hardly unfastened her hair, and thrown a loose gown about her, before there was a knock at the door, and Mrs Sharp's voice said – 'Miss Tina, my lady wants to know if you're ill.'

Caterina opened the door and said, 'Thank you, dear Mrs Sharp; I have a bad headache; please tell my lady I felt it come on after singing.'

'Then, goodness me! why arn't you in bed, istid o' standing shivering there, fit to catch your death? Come, let me fasten up your hair and tuck you up warm.'

'O no, thank you; I shall really be in bed very soon. Goodnight, dear Sharpy; don't scold; I will be good, and get into bed.'

Caterina kissed her old friend coaxingly, but Mrs Sharp was not to be 'come over' in that way, and insisted on seeing her former charge in bed, taking away the candle that the poor child had wanted to keep as a companion. But it was impossible to lie there long with that beating heart; and the little white figure was soon out of bed again, seeking relief in the very sense of chill and uncomfort. It was light enough for her to see about her room, for the moon, nearly at full, was riding high in the heavens among scattered hurrying clouds. Caterina drew aside the window-curtain, and, sitting with her forehead pressed against the cold pane, looked out on the wide stretch of park and lawn.

How dreary the moonlight is! robbed of all its tenderness and repose by the hard driving wind. The trees are harassed by that tossing motion, when they would like to be at rest; the shivering grass makes her quake with sympathetic cold; and the willows by the pool, bent low and white under that invisible harshness, seem agitated and helpless like herself. But she loves the scene the better for its sadness: there is some pity in it. It is not like that hard unfeeling happiness of lovers, flaunting in the eyes of misery.

She set her teeth tight against the window-frame, and the tears fell thick and fast. She was so thankful she could cry, for the mad passion she had felt when her eyes were dry frightened her. If that dreadful feeling were to come on when Lady Cheverel was present, she should never be able to contain herself.

Then there was Sir Christopher – so good to her – so happy about Anthony's marriage, and all the while she had these wicked feelings.

'O, I cannot help it, I cannot help it!' she said in a loud whisper between her sobs. 'O God, have pity upon me!'

In this way Tina wore out the long hours of the windy moonlight, till at last, with weary aching limbs, she lay down in bed again, and slept from mere exhaustion.

While this poor little heart was being bruised with a weight too heavy for it, Nature was holding on her calm inexorable way, in unmoved and terrible beauty. The stars were rushing in their eternal courses; the tides swelled to the level of the last expectant weed; the sun was making brilliant day to busy nations on the other side of the swift earth. The stream of human thought and deed was hurrying and broadening onward. The astronomer was at his telescope; the great ships were labouring over the waves; the toiling eagerness of commerce, the fierce spirit of revolution, were only ebbing in brief rest; and sleepless states-men were dreading the possible crisis of the morrow. What were our little Tina and her trouble in this mighty torrent, rushing from one awful unknown to another? Lighter than the smallest centre of quivering life in the waterdrop, hidden and uncared for as the pulse of anguish in the breast of the tiniest bird that has fluttered down to its nest with the long-sought food, and has found the nest torn and empty.

## 6

The next morning, when Caterina was waked from her heavy sleep by Martha bringing in the warm water, the sun was shining, the wind had abated, and those hours of suffering in the night seemed unreal and dreamlike, in spite of weary limbs and aching eyes. She got up and began to dress with a strange feeling of insensibility, as if nothing could make her cry again, and she even felt a sort of longing to be downstairs in the midst of company, that she might get rid of this benumbed condition by contact.

There are few of us that are not rather ashamed of our sins and follies as we look out on the blessed morning sunlight, which comes to us like a bright-winged angel beckoning us to quit the old path of vanity that stretches its dreary length behind us, and Tina, little as she knew about doctrines and theories, seemed to herself to have been both foolish and wicked yesterday. Today she would try to be good, and when she knelt down to say her short prayer – the very form she had learned by heart when she was ten years old – she added, 'O God, help me to bear it!'

That day the prayer seemed to be answered, for after some remarks on her pale looks at breakfast, Caterina passed the morning quietly, Miss Assher and Captain Wybrow being out on a riding excursion. In the evening there was a dinner-party, and after Caterina had sung a little, Lady Cheverel remembering that she was ailing, sent her to bed, where she soon sank into a deep sleep. Body and mind must renew their force to suffer as well as to enjoy.

On the morrow, however, it was rainy, and everyone must stay indoors, so it was resolved that the guests should be taken over the house by Sir Christopher, to hear the story of the architectural alterations, the family portraits, and the family relics. All the party, except Mr Gilfil, were in the drawing room when the proposition was made, and when Miss Assher rose to go, she looked towards Captain Wybrow, expecting to see him rise too; but he kept his seat near the fire, turning his eyes towards the newspaper which he had been holding unread in his hand.

'Are you not coming, Anthony?' said Lady Cheverel, noticing Miss Assher's look of expectation.

'I think not, if you'll excuse me,' he answered, rising and opening the door; 'I feel a little chilled this morning, and I am afraid of the cold rooms and draughts.'

Miss Assher reddened, but said nothing, and passed on, Lady Cheverel accompanying her.

Caterina was seated at work in the oriel window. It was the first time she and Anthony had been alone together, and she had thought before that he wished to avoid her. But now, surely, he wanted to speak to her – he wanted to say something kind. Presently he rose from his seat near the fire, and placed himself on the ottoman opposite to her.

'Well, Tina, and how have you been all this long time?' Both the tone and the words were an offence to her; the tone was so different from the old one, the words were so cold and unmeaning. She answered, with a little bitterness, 'I think you needn't ask. It doesn't make much difference to you.'

'Is that the kindest thing you have to say to me after my long absence?'

'I don't know why you should expect me to say kind things.'

Captain Wybrow was silent. He wished very much to avoid allusions to the past or comments on the present. And yet he wished to be well with Caterina. He would have liked to caress her, make her presents, and have her think him very kind to her. But these women are plaguy perverse! There's no bringing them to look rationally at anything. At last he said, 'I hoped you would think all the better of me, Tina, for doing as I have done, instead of bearing malice towards me. I hoped you would see that it is the best thing for everyone – the best for your happiness too.'

'O pray don't make love to Miss Assher for the sake of my happiness,' answered Tina.

At this moment the door opened, and Miss Assher entered, to fetch her reticule, which lay on the harpsichord. She gave a keen glance at Caterina, whose face was flushed, and saying to Captain Wybrow with a slight sneer, 'Since you are so chill I wonder you like to sit in the window,' left the room again immediately.

The lover did not appear much discomposed, but sat quiet a little longer, and then, seating himself on the music-stool, drew it near to Caterina, and, taking her hand, said, 'Come, Tina, look kindly at me, and let us be friends. I shall always be your friend.'

'Thank you,' said Caterina, drawing away her hand. 'You are very generous. But pray move away. Miss Assher may come in again.'

'Miss Assher be hanged!' said Anthony, feeling the fascination of old habit returning on him in his proximity to Caterina. He put his arm round her waist, and leaned his cheek down to hers. The lips couldn't help meeting after that; but the next moment, with heart swelling and tears rising, Caterina burst away from him, and rushed out of the room.

7

Caterina tore herself from Anthony with the desperate effort of one who has just self-recollection enough left to be conscious that the fumes of charcoal will master his senses unless he bursts a way for himself to the fresh air, but when she reached her own room, she was still too intoxicated with that momentary revival of old emotions, too much agitated by the sudden return of tenderness in her lover, to know whether pain or pleasure predominated. It was as if a miracle had happened in her little world of feeling, and made the future all vague – a dim morning haze of possibilities, instead of the sombre wintry daylight and clear rigid outline of painful certainty.

She felt the need of rapid movement. She must walk out in spite of the rain. Happily, there was a thin place in the curtain of clouds which seemed to promise that now, about noon, the day had a mind to clear up. Caterina thought to herself, 'I will walk to the Mosslands, and carry Mr Bates the comforter I have made for him, and then Lady Cheverel will not wonder so much at my going out.' At the hall door she found

Rupert, the old bloodhound, stationed on the mat, with the determination that the first person who was sensible enough to take a walk that morning should have the honour of his approbation and society. As he thrust his great black and tawny head under her hand, and wagged his tail with vigorous eloquence, and reached the climax of his welcome by jumping up to lick her face, which was at a convenient licking height for him, Caterina felt quite grateful to the old dog for his friendliness. Animals are such agreeable friends – they ask no questions, they pass no criticisms.

The 'Mosslands' was a remote part of the grounds, encircled by the little stream issuing from the pool, and certainly, for a wet day, Caterina could hardly have chosen a less suitable walk, for though the rain was abating, and presently ceased altogether, there was still a smart shower falling from the trees that arched over the greater part of her way. But she found just the desired relief from her feverish excitement in labouring along the wet paths with an umbrella that made her arm ache. This amount of exertion was to her tiny body what a day's hunting often was to Mr Gilfil, who at times had *his* fits of jealousy and sadness to get rid of, and wisely had recourse to nature's innocent opium – fatigue.

When Caterina reached the pretty arched wooden bridge that formed the only entrance to the Mosslands for any but webbed feet, the sun had mastered the clouds, and was shining through the boughs of the tall elms that made a deep nest for the gardener's cottage – turning the raindrops into diamonds, and inviting the nasturtium flowers creeping over the porch and low-thatched roof to lift up their flame-coloured heads once more. The rooks were cawing with many-voiced monotony, apparently – by a remarkable approximation to human intelligence – finding great conversational resources in the change of weather. The mossy turf, studded with the broad blades of marsh-loving plants, told that Mr Bates's nest was rather damp in the best of weather, but he was of opinion that a little external moisture would hurt no man who was not perversely neglectful of that obvious and providential antidote, rum-and-water.

Caterina loved this nest. Every object in it, every sound that haunted it, had been familiar to her from the days when she had been carried thither on Mr Bates's arm, making little cawing noises to imitate the rooks, clapping her hands at the green frogs leaping in the moist grass, and fixing grave eyes on the gardener's fowls cluck-clucking under their pens. And now the spot looked prettier to her than ever; it was so out of the way of Miss Assher, with her brilliant beauty, and personal claims, and small civil remarks. She thought Mr Bates would not be come into his dinner yet, so she would sit down and wait for him.

But she was mistaken. Mr Bates was seated in his armchair, with his pocket handkerchief thrown over his face, as the most eligible mode of passing away those superfluous hours between meals when the weather drives a man indoors. Roused by the furious barking of his chained bulldog, he descried his little favourite approaching, and forthwith presented himself at the doorway, looking disproportionately tall compared with the height of his cottage. The bulldog, meanwhile, unbent from the severity of his official demeanour, and commenced a friendly interchange of ideas with Rupert.

Mr Bates's hair was now grey, but his frame was none the less stalwart, and his face looked all the redder, making an artistic contrast with the deep blue of his cotton neckerchief, and of his linen apron twisted into a girdle round his waist.

'Why, dang my boottons, Miss Tiny,' he exclaimed, 'hoo coom ye to coom oot dabblin' your faet laike a little Muscovy duck, sich a day as this? Not but what ai'm delaighted to sae ye. Here Hesther,' he called to his old humpbacked housekeeper, 'tek the young ledy's oombrella an' spread it oot to dray. Coom, coom in, Miss Tiny, an' set ye doon by the faire an' dray yer faet, an' hev summat warm to kape ye from ketchin' coold.'

Mr Bates led the way, stooping under the doorplaces, into his small sitting room, and, shaking the patchwork cushion in his armchair, moved it to within a good roasting distance of the blazing fire.

'Thank you, uncle Bates' (Caterina kept up her childish epithets for her friends, and this was one of them); 'not quite so close to the fire, for I am warm with walking.'

'Eh, but yer shoes are faine an' wet, an' ye must put up yer faet on the fender. Rare big faet, baint 'em? – aboot the saize of a good big spoon. I woonder ye can mek a shift to stan' on 'em. Now, what'll ye hev to warm yer insaide? – a drop o' hot elder wain, now?'

'No, not anything to drink, thank you; it isn't very long since breakfast,' said Caterina, drawing out the comforter from her deep pocket. Pockets were capacious in those days. 'Look here, uncle Bates, here is what I came to bring you. I made it on purpose for you. You must wear it this winter, and give your red one to old Brooks.'

'Eh, Miss Tiny, this *is* a beauty. An' ye made it all wi' yer little fingers for an old feller laike mae! I tek it very kaind on ye, an' I belave ye I'll wear it, and be prood on't too. These sthraipes, blue an' whaite, now, they mek it uncommon pritty.'

'Yes, that will suit your complexion, you know, better than the old scarlet one. I know Mrs Sharp will be more in love with you than ever when she sees you in the new one.'

'My complexion, ye little roogue! ye're a laughin' at me. But talkin' o' complexions, what a beautiful colour the bride as is to be has on her cheeks! Dang my boottons! she looks faine and handsome o' hossback – sits as upraight as a dart, wi' a figure like a statty! Misthress Sharp has promised to put me behind one o' the doors when the ladies are comin' doon to dinner, so as I may sae the young un i' full dress, wi' all her curls an' that. Misthress Sharp says she's almost beautifuller nor my ledy was when she was yoong; an' I think ye'll noot faind man i' the counthry as'll coom up to that.'

'Yes, Miss Assher is very handsome,' said Caterina, rather faintly, feeling the sense of her own insignificance returning at this picture of the impression Miss Assher made on others.

'Well, an' I hope she's good too, an'll mek a good naice to Sir Cristhifer an' my ledy. Misthress Griffin, the maid, says as she's rether tatchy and find-fautin' aboot her cloothes, laike. But she's yoong – she's yoong; that'll wear off when she's got a hoosband, an' children, an' summat else to think on. Sir Cristhifer's fain an' delaighted, I can see. He says to me th' other mornin', says he, "Well, Bates, what do you think of your young misthress as is to be?" An' I says, "Whay, yer honour, I think she's as fain a lass as iver I set eyes on; an' I wish the Captain luck in a fain family, an' your honour laife an' health to see't." Mr Warren says as the masther's all for forrardin' the weddin', an' it'll very laike be afore the autumn's oot.'

As Mr Bates ran on, Caterina felt something like a painful contraction at her heart. 'Yes,' she said, rising, 'I dare say it will. Sir Christopher is very anxious for it. But I must go, uncle Bates; Lady Cheverel will be wanting me, and it is your dinner time.'

'Nay, my dinner doon't sinnify a bit; but I moosn't kaep ye if my ledy wants ye. Though I hevn't thanked ye half anoof for the comfiter – the wrapraskil, as they call't. My feckins, it's a beauty. But ye look very whaite and sadly, Miss Tiny; I doubt ye're poorly; an' this walking i' th' wet isn't good for ye.'

'O yes, it is indeed,' said Caterina, hastening out, and taking up her umbrella from the kitchen floor. 'I must really go now; so goodbye.'

She tripped off, calling Rupert, while the good gardener, his hands thrust deep in his pockets, stood looking after her and shaking his head with rather a melancholy air.

'She gets moor nesh and dillicat than iver,' he said, half to himself and half to Hester. 'I shouldn't woonder if she fades away laike them cyclamens as I transplanted. She puts me i' maind on 'em somehow, hangin' on their little thin stalks, so whaite an' tinder.'

The poor little thing made her way back, no longer hungering for the cold moist air as a counteractive of inward excitement, but with a chill at her heart that made the outward chill only depressing. The golden sunlight beamed through the dripping boughs like a Shekinah, or visible divine presence, and the birds were chirping and trilling their new autumnal songs so sweetly, it seemed as if their throats, as well as the air, were all the clearer for the rain, but Caterina moved through all this joy and beauty like a poor wounded leveret painfully dragging its little body through the sweet clover-tufts – for it, sweet in vain. Mr Bates's words about Sir Christopher's joy, Miss Assher's beauty, and the nearness of the wedding, had come upon her like the pressure of a cold hand, rousing her from confused dozing to a perception of hard, familiar realities. It is so with emotional natures whose thoughts are no more than the fleeting shadows cast by feeling: to them words are facts, and even when known to be false, have a mastery over their smiles and tears. Caterina entered her own room again, with no other change from her former state of despondency and wretchedness than an additional sense of injury from Anthony. His behaviour towards her in the morning was a new wrong. To snatch a caress when she justly claimed an expression of penitence, of regret, of sympathy, was to make more light of her than ever.

## 8

That evening Miss Assher seemed to carry herself with unusual haughtiness, and was coldly observant of Caterina. There was unmistakably thunder in the air. Captain Wybrow appeared to take the matter very easily, and was inclined to brave it out by paying more than ordinary attention to Caterina. Mr Gilfil had induced her to play a game at draughts with him, Lady Assher being seated at picquet with Sir Christopher, and Miss Assher in determined conversation with Lady Cheverel. Anthony, thus left as an odd unit, sauntered up to Caterina's chair, and leaned behind her, watching the game. Tina, with all the remembrances of the morning thick upon her, felt her cheeks becoming more and more crimson, and at last said impatiently, 'I wish you would go away.'

This happened directly under the view of Miss Assher, who saw Caterina's reddening cheeks, saw that she said something impatiently, and that Captain Wybrow moved away in consequence. There was another person, too, who had noticed this incident with strong interest, and who was moreover aware that Miss Assher not only saw, but keenly observed what was passing. That other person was Mr Gilfil, and he drew some painful conclusions that heightened his anxiety for Caterina.

The next morning, in spite of the fine weather, Miss Assher declined riding, and Lady Cheverel, perceiving that there was something wrong between the lovers, took care that they should be left together in the drawing room. Miss Assher, seated on the sofa near the fire, was busy with some fancy-work, in which she seemed bent on making great progress this morning. Captain Wybrow sat opposite with a newspaper in his hand, from which he obligingly read extracts with an elaborately easy air, wilfully unconscious of the contemptuous silence with which she pursued her filigree work. At length he put down the paper, which he could no longer pretend not to have exhausted, and Miss Assher then said, 'You seem to be on very intimate terms with Miss Sarti.'

'With Tina? oh yes; she has always been the pet of the house, you know. We have been quite brother and sister together.'

'Sisters don't generally colour so very deeply when their brothers approach them.'

'Does she colour? I never noticed it. But she's a timid little thing.'

'It would be much better if you would not be so hypocritical, Captain Wybrow. I am confident there has been some flirtation between you. Miss Sarti, in her position, would never speak to you with the petulance she did last night, if you had not given her some kind of claim on you.'

'My dear Beatrice, now do be reasonable; do ask yourself what earthly probability there is that I should think of flirting with poor little Tina. *Is* there anything about her to attract that sort of attention? She is more child than woman. One thinks of her as a little girl to be petted and played with.'

'Pray, what were you playing at with her yesterday morning, when I came in unexpectedly, and her cheeks were flushed, and her hands trembling?

'Yesterday morning? – O, I remember. You know I always tease her about Gilfil, who is over head and ears in love with her, and she is angry at that – perhaps, because she likes him. They were old play-fellows years before I came here, and Sir Christopher has set his heart on their marrying.'

'Captain Wybrow, you are very false. It had nothing to do with Mr Gilfil that she coloured last night when you leaned over her chair. You might just as well be candid. If your own mind is not made up, pray do no violence to yourself. I am quite ready to give way to Miss Sarti's superior attractions. Understand that, so far as I am concerned, you are perfectly at liberty. I decline any share in the affection of a man who forfeits my respect by duplicity.'

In saying this Miss Assher rose, and was sweeping haughtily out of the room, when Captain Wybrow placed himself before her, and took her hand. 'Dear, dear Beatrice, be patient; do not judge me so rashly. Sit down again, sweet,' he added in a pleading voice, pressing both her hands between his, and leading her back to the sofa, where he sat down beside her. Miss Assher was not unwilling to be led back or to listen, but she retained her cold and haughty expression.

'Can you not trust me, Beatrice? Can you not believe me, although there may be things I am unable to explain?'

'Why should there be anything you are unable to explain? An honour-able man will not be placed in circumstances which he cannot explain to

67

the woman he seeks to make his wife. He will not ask her to *believe* that he acts properly; he will let her *know* that he does so. Let me go, sir.'

She attempted to rise, but he passed his hand round her waist and detained her.

'Now, Beatrice dear,' he said imploringly, 'can you not understand that there are things a man doesn't like to talk about – secrets that he must keep for the sake of others, and not for his own sake? Everything that relates to myself you may ask me, but do not ask me to tell other people's secrets. Don't you understand me?'

'O yes,' said Miss Assher scornfully, 'I understand. Whenever you make love to a woman – that is her secret, which you are bound to keep for her. But it is folly to be talking in this way, Captain Wybrow. It is very plain that there is some relation more than friendship between you and Miss Sarti. Since you cannot explain that relation, there is no more to be said between us.'

'Confound it, Beatrice! you'll drive me mad. Can a fellow help a girl's falling in love with him? Such things are always happening, but men don't talk of them. These fancies will spring up without the slightest foundation, especially when a woman sees few people; they die out again when there is no encouragement. If you could like me, you ought not to be surprised that other people can; you ought to think the better of them for it.'

'You mean to say, then, that Miss Sarti is in love with you, without your ever having made love to her.'

'Do not press me to say such things, dearest. It is enough that you know I love you – that I am devoted to you. You naughty queen, you, you know there is no chance for anyone else where you are. You are only tormenting me, to prove your power over me. But don't be too cruel, for you know they say I have another heart disease besides love, and these scenes bring on terrible palpitations.'

'But I must have an answer to this one question,' said Miss Assher, a little softened: 'Has there been, or is there, any love on your side towards Miss Sarti? I have nothing to do with her feelings, but I have a right to know yours.'

'I like Tina very much; who would not like such a little simple thing? You would not wish me not to like her? But love – that is a very different affair. One has a brotherly affection for such a woman as Tina, but it is another sort of woman that one loves.'

These last words were made doubly significant by a look of tenderness, and a kiss imprinted on the hand Captain Wybrow held in his. Miss Assher was conquered. It was so far from probable that Anthony should love that pale insignificant little thing – so highly probable that he should adore the beautiful Miss Assher. On the whole, it was rather gratifying that other women should be languishing for her handsome lover; he really was an exquisite creature. Poor Miss Sarti! Well, she would get over it.

Captain Wybrow saw his advantage. 'Come, sweet love,' he continued, 'let us talk no more about unpleasant things. You will keep Tina's secret, and be very kind to her – won't you? – for my sake. But you will ride out now? See what a glorious day it is for riding. Let me order the horses. I'm terribly in want of the air. Come, give me one forgiving kiss, and say you will go.'

Miss Assher complied with the double request, and then went to equip herself for the ride, while her lover walked to the stables.


9


Meanwhile Mr Gilfil, who had a heavy weight on his mind, had watched for the moment when, the two elder ladies having driven out, Caterina would probably be alone in Lady Cheverel's sitting room. He went up and knocked at the door.

'Come in,' said the sweet mellow voice, always thrilling to him as the sound of rippling water to the thirsty.

He entered and found Caterina standing in some confusion as if she had been startled from a reverie. She felt relieved when she saw it was Maynard, but, the next moment, felt a little pettish that he should have come to interrupt and frighten her.

'Oh, it is you, Maynard! Do you want Lady Cheverel?'

'No, Caterina,' he answered gravely; 'I want you. I have something very particular to say to you. Will you let me sit down with you for half an hour?'

'Yes, dear old preacher,' said Caterina, sitting down with an air of weariness; 'what is it?'

Mr Gilfil placed himself opposite to her, and said, 'I hope you will not be hurt, Caterina, by what I am going to say to you. I do not speak from any other feelings than real affection and anxiety for you. I put everything else out of the question. You know you are more to me than all the world, but I will not thrust before you a feeling that you are unable to return. I speak to you as a brother – the old Maynard that used to scold you for getting your fishing line tangled ten years ago. You will not believe that I have any mean, selfish motive in mentioning things that are painful to you?'

'No; I know you are very good,' said Caterina, abstractedly.

'From what I saw yesterday evening,' Mr Gilfil went on, hesitating and colouring slightly, 'I am led to fear – pray forgive me if I am wrong, Caterina – that you – that Captain Wybrow is base enough still to trifle with your feelings, that he still allows himself to behave to you as no man ought who is the declared lover of another woman.'

'What do you mean, Maynard?' said Caterina, with anger flashing from her eyes. 'Do you mean that I let him make love to me? What right have you to think that of me? What do you mean that you saw yesterday evening?'

'Do not be angry, Caterina. I don't suspect you of doing wrong. I only suspect that heartless puppy of behaving so as to keep awake feelings in you that not only destroy your own peace of mind, but may lead to very bad consequences with regard to others. I want to warn you that Miss Assher has her eyes open on what passes between you and Captain Wybrow, and I feel sure she is getting jealous of you. Pray be very careful, Caterina, and try to behave with politeness and indifference to him. You must see by this time that he is not worth the feeling you have given him. He's more disturbed at his pulse beating one too many in a minute, than at all the misery he has caused you by his foolish trifling.'

'You ought not to speak so of him, Maynard,' said Caterina, passionately. 'He is not what you think. He *did* care for me; he *did* love me; only he wanted to do what his uncle wished.'

'O to be sure! I know it is only from the most virtuous motives that he does what is convenient to himself.'

Mr Gilfil paused. He felt that he was getting irritated, and defeating his own object. Presently he continued in a calm and affectionate tone.

'I will say no more about what I think of him, Caterina. But whether he loved you or not, his position now with Miss Assher is such that any love you may cherish for him can bring nothing but misery. God knows, I don't expect you to leave off loving him at a moment's notice. Time and absence, and trying to do what is right, are the only cures. If it were not that Sir Christopher and Lady Cheverel would be displeased and puzzled at your wishing to leave home just now, I would beg you to pay a visit to my sister. She and her husband are good creatures, and would make their house a home to you. But I could not urge the thing just now without giving a special reason, and what is most of all to be dreaded is the raising of any suspicion in Sir Christopher's mind of what has happened in the past, or of your present feelings. You think so too, don't you, Tina?'

Mr Gilfil paused again, but Caterina said nothing. She was looking away from him, out of the window, and her eyes were filling with tears. He rose, and, advancing a little towards her, held out his hand and said, 'Forgive me, Caterina, for intruding on your feelings in this way. I was so afraid you might not be aware how Miss Assher watched you. Remember, I entreat you, that the peace of the whole family depends on your power of governing yourself. Only say you forgive me before I go.'

'Dear, good Maynard,' she said, stretching out her little hand, and taking two of his large fingers in her grasp, while her tears flowed fast; 'I am very cross to you. But my heart is breaking. I don't know what I do. Goodbye.'

He stooped down, kissed the little hand, and then left the room.

'The cursed scoundrel!' he muttered between his teeth, as he closed the door behind him. 'If it were not for Sir Christopher, I should like to pound him into paste to poison puppies like himself.'

## 10

That evening Captain Wybrow, returning from a long ride with Miss Assher, went up to his dressing room, and seated himself with an air of considerable lassitude before his mirror. The reflection there presented of his exquisite self was certainly paler and more worn than usual, and might excuse the anxiety with which he first felt his pulse, and then laid his hand on his heart.

'It's a devil of a position this for a man to be in,' was the train of his thought, as he kept his eyes fixed on the glass, while he leaned back in his chair, and crossed his hands behind his head; 'between two jealous women, and both of them as ready to take fire as tinder. And in my state of health, too! I should be glad enough to run away from the whole affair, and go off to some lotus-eating place or other where there are no women, or only women who are too sleepy to be jealous. Here am I, doing nothing to please myself, trying to do the best thing for everybody else, and all the comfort I get is to have fire shot at me from women's eyes, and venom spurted at me from women's tongues. If Beatrice takes another jealous fit into her head – and it's likely enough, Tina is so unmanageable – I don't know what storm she may raise. And any hitch in this marriage, especially of that sort, might be a fatal business for the old gentleman. I wouldn't have such a blow fall upon him for a great deal. Besides, a man must be married some time in his life, and I could hardly do better than marry Beatrice. She's an uncommonly fine woman, and I'm really very fond of her, and as I shall let her have her own way, her temper won't signify much. I wish the wedding was over and done with, for this fuss doesn't suit me at all. I haven't been half so well lately. That scene about Tina this morning quite upset me. Poor little Tina! What a little simpleton it was, to set her heart on me in that way! But she ought to see how impossible it is that things should be different. If she would but understand how kindly I feel towards her, and make up her mind to look on me as a friend – but that it what one never can get a woman to do. Beatrice is very good-natured; I'm sure she would be kind to the little thing. It would be a great comfort if Tina would take to Gilfil, if it were only in anger against me. He'd make her a capital husband, and I should like to see the little grasshopper happy. If I had been in a different position, I would certainly have married her myself: but that was out of the question with my responsibilities to Sir Christopher. I think a little persuasion from my uncle would bring her to accept Gilfil; I know she would never be able to oppose my uncle's wishes. And if they were once married, she's such a loving little thing, she would soon be billing and cooing with him as if she had never known me. It would certainly be the best thing for her happiness if that marriage were hastened. Heigho! Those are lucky fellows that have no women falling in love with them. It's a confounded responsibility.'

At this point in his meditations he turned his head a little, so as to get a three-quarter view of his face. Clearly it was the '*dono infelice della bellezza*'[30] that laid these onerous duties upon him – an idea that naturally suggested that he should ring for his valet.

For the next few days, however, there was such a cessation of threatening symptoms as to allay the anxiety both of Captain Wybrow and Mr Gilfil. All earthly things have their lull: even on nights when the most unappeasable wind is raging, there will be a moment of stillness before it crashes among the boughs again, and storms against the windows, and howls like a thousand lost demons through the keyholes.

Miss Assher appeared to be in the highest good humour; Captain Wybrow was more assiduous than usual, and was very circumspect in his behaviour to Caterina, on whom Miss Assher bestowed unwonted attentions. The weather was brilliant; there were riding excursions in the mornings and dinner-parties in the evenings. Consultations in the library between Sir Christopher and Lady Assher seemed to be leading to a satisfactory result, and it was understood that this visit at Cheverel Manor would terminate in another fortnight, when the preparations for the wedding would be carried forward with all despatch at Farleigh. The Baronet seemed every day more radiant. Accustomed to view people who entered into his plans by the pleasant light that his own strong will and bright hopefulness were always casting on the future, he saw nothing but personal charms and promising domestic qualities in Miss Assher, whose quickness of eye and taste in externals formed a real ground of sympathy between her and Sir Christopher. Lady Cheverel's enthusiasm never rose above the temperate mark of calm satisfaction, and, having quite her share of the critical acumen that characterises the mutual estimates of the fair sex, she had a more moderate opinion of Miss Assher's qualities. She suspected that the fair Beatrice had a sharp and imperious temper; and being herself, on principle and by habitual self-command, the most deferential of wives, she noticed with disapproval Miss Assher's occasional air of authority towards Captain Wybrow. A proud woman who has learned to submit carries all her pride to the reinforcement of her submission, and looks down with severe superiority on all feminine assumption as 'unbecoming'. Lady Cheverel, however, confined her criticisms to the privacy of her own thoughts, and, with a reticence that I fear may seem incredible, did not use them as a means of disturbing her husband's complacency.

And Caterina? How did she pass these sunny autumn days, in which the skies seemed to be smiling on the family gladness? To her the change in Miss Assher's manner was unaccountable. Those compassionate attentions, those smiling condescensions, were torture to Caterina, who was constantly tempted to repulse them with anger. She thought, 'Perhaps Anthony has told her to be kind to poor Tina.' This was an insult. He ought to have known that the mere presence of Miss Assher was painful to her, that Miss Assher's smiles scorched her, that Miss Assher's kind words were like poison stings inflaming her to madness. And he – Anthony – he was evidently repenting of the tenderness he had been betrayed into that morning in the drawing room. He was cold and distant and civil to her, to ward off Beatrice's suspicions, and Beatrice could be so gracious now, because she was sure of Anthony's entire devotion. Well! and so it ought to be – and she ought not to wish it otherwise. And yet – oh, he *was* cruel to her. She could never have behaved so to him. To make her love him so – to speak such tender words – to give her such caresses, and then to behave as if such things had never been. He had given her the poison that seemed so sweet while she was drinking it, and now it was in her blood, and she was helpless.

With this tempest pent up in her bosom, the poor child went up to her room every night, and there it all burst forth. There, with loud whispers and sobs, restlessly pacing up and down, lying on the hard floor, courting cold and weariness, she told to the pitiful listening night the anguish that she could pour into no mortal ear. But always sleep came at last, and always in the morning the reactive calm that enabled her to live through the day.

It is amazing how long a young frame will go on battling with this sort of secret wretchedness, and yet show no traces of the conflict for any but

74

sympathetic eyes. The very delicacy of Caterina's usual appearance, her natural paleness and habitually quiet mouse-like ways, made any symptoms of fatigue and suffering less noticeable. And her singing – the one thing in which she ceased to be passive, and became prominent – lost none of its energy. She herself sometimes wondered how it was that, whether she felt sad or angry, crushed with the sense of Anthony's indifference, or burning with impatience under Miss Assher's attentions, it was always a relief to her to sing. Those full deep notes she sent forth seemed to be lifting the pain from her heart – seemed to be carrying away the madness from her brain.

Thus Lady Cheverel noticed no change in Caterina, and it was only Mr Gilfil who discerned with anxiety the feverish spot that sometimes rose on her cheek, the deepening violet tint under her eyes, and the strange absent glance, the unhealthy glitter of the beautiful eyes themselves. But those agitated nights were producing a more fatal effect than was represented by these slight outward changes.

## 11

The following Sunday, the morning being rainy, it was determined that the family should not go to Cumbermoor Church as usual, but that Mr Gilfil, who had only an afternoon service at his curacy, should conduct the morning service in the chapel.

Just before the appointed hour of eleven, Caterina came down into the drawing room, looking so unusually ill as to call forth an anxious enquiry from Lady Cheverel, who, on learning that she had a severe headache, insisted that she should not attend service, and at once packed her up comfortably on a sofa near the fire, putting a volume of Tillotson's Sermons[31] into her hands – as appropriate reading, if Caterina should feel equal to that means of edification.

Excellent medicine for the mind are the good Archbishop's sermons, but a medicine, unhappily, not suited to Tina's case. She sat with the book open on her knees, her dark eyes fixed vacantly on the portrait of that handsome Lady Cheverel, wife of the notable Sir Anthony. She gazed at the picture without thinking of it, and the fair blonde dame seemed to look down on her with that benignant unconcern, that mild wonder, with which happy self-possessed women are apt to look down on their agitated and weaker sisters.

Caterina was thinking of the near future – of the wedding that was so soon to come – of all she would have to live through in the next months.

'I wish I could be very ill, and die before then,' she thought. 'When people get very ill, they don't mind about things. Poor Patty Richards looked so happy when she was in a decline. She didn't seem to care any more about her lover that she was engaged to be married to, and she liked the smell of the flowers so, that I used to take her. O, if I could but like anything – if I could but think about anything else! If these dreadful feelings would go away, I wouldn't mind about not being happy. I wouldn't want anything – and I could do what would please Sir Christopher and Lady Cheverel. But when that rage and anger comes into me, I don't know what to do. I don't feel the ground under me; I only feel my head and heart beating, and it seems as if I must do something dreadful. O! I wonder if anyone ever felt like me before. I must be very wicked. But God will have pity on me; He knows all I have to bear.'

In this way the time wore on till Tina heard the sound of voices along the passage, and became conscious that the volume of Tillotson had slipped on the floor. She had only just picked it up, and seen with alarm that the pages were bent, when Lady Assher, Beatrice, and Captain Wybrow entered, all with that brisk and cheerful air that a sermon is often observed to produce when it is quite finished.

Lady Assher at once came and seated herself by Caterina. Her ladyship had been considerably refreshed by a doze, and was in great force for monologue.

'Well, my dear Miss Sarti, and how do you feel now? – a little better, I see. I thought you would be, sitting quietly here. These headaches, now, are all from weakness. You must not over-exert yourself, and you must take bitters. I used to have just the same sort of headaches when I was your age, and old Dr Samson used to say to my mother, "Madam, what your daughter suffers from is weakness." He was such a curious old man, was Dr Samson. But I wish you could have heard the sermon this morning. Such an excellent sermon! It was about the ten virgins: five of them were foolish, and five were clever, you know; and Mr Gilfil explained all that. What a very pleasant young man he is! so very quiet and agreeable, and such a good hand at whist. I wish we had him at Farleigh. Sir John would have liked him beyond anything; he is so good-tempered at cards, and he was such a man for cards, was Sir John. And our rector is a very irritable man; he can't bear to lose his money at cards. I don't think a clergyman ought to mind about losing his money; do you? – do you now?'

'O pray, Lady Assher,' interposed Beatrice, in her usual tone of superiority, 'do not weary poor Caterina with such uninteresting questions. Your head seems very bad still, dear,' she continued, in a condoling tone, to Caterina; 'do take my vinaigrette,[32] and keep it in your pocket. It will perhaps refresh you now and then.'

'No, thank you,' answered Caterina; 'I will not take it away from you.'

'Indeed, dear, I never use it; you must take it,' Miss Assher persisted, holding it close to Tina's hand. Tina coloured deeply, pushed the vinaigrette away with some impatience, and said, 'Thank you, I never use those things. I don't like vinaigrettes.'

Miss Assher returned the vinaigrette to her pocket in surprise and haughty silence, and Captain Wybrow, who had looked on in some alarm, said hastily, 'See! it is quite bright out of doors now. There is time for a walk before luncheon. Come, Beatrice, put on your hat and cloak, and let us have half an hour's walk on the gravel.'

'Yes, do, my dear,' said Lady Assher, 'and I will go and see if Sir Christopher is having his walk in the gallery.'

As soon as the door had closed behind the two ladies, Captain Wybrow, standing with his back to the fire, turned towards Caterina, and said in a tone of earnest remonstrance, 'My dear Caterina. Let me beg of you to exercise more control over your feelings; you are really rude to Miss Assher, and I can see that she is quite hurt. Consider how strange your behaviour must appear to her. She will wonder what can be the cause of it. Come, dear Tina,' he added, approaching her, and attempting to take her hand; 'for your own sake let me entreat you to receive her attentions politely. She really feels very kindly towards you, and I should be so happy to see you friends.'

Caterina was already in such a state of diseased susceptibility that the most innocent words from Captain Wybrow would have been irritating to her, as the whirr of the most delicate wing will afflict a nervous patient. But this tone of benevolent remonstrance was intolerable. He had inflicted a great and unrepented injury on her, and now he assumed an air of benevolence towards her. This was a new outrage. His profession of goodwill was insolence.

Caterina snatched away her hand and said indignantly, 'Leave me to myself, Captain Wybrow! I do not disturb you.'

'Caterina, why will you be so violent – so unjust to me? It is for you that I feel anxious. Miss Assher has already noticed how strange your behaviour is both to her and me, and it puts me into a very difficult position. What can I say to her?'

'Say?' Caterina burst forth with intense bitterness, rising, and moving towards the door; 'say that I am a poor silly girl, and have fallen in love with you, and am jealous of her, but that you have never had any feeling but pity for me – you have never behaved with anything more than friendliness to me. Tell her that, and she will think all the better of you.'

Tina uttered this as the bitterest sarcasm her ideas would furnish her with, not having the faintest suspicion that the sarcasm derived any of its bitterness from truth. Underneath all her sense of wrong, which was rather instinctive than reflective – underneath all the madness of her jealousy, and her ungovernable impulses of resentment and vindictiveness – underneath all this scorching passion there were still left some hidden crystal dews of trust, of self-reproof, of belief that Anthony was trying to do the right. Love had not all gone to feed the fires of hatred. Tina still trusted that Anthony felt more for her than he seemed to feel; she was still far from suspecting him of a wrong that a woman resents even more than inconstancy. And she threw out this taunt simply as the most intense expression she could find for the anger of the moment.

As she stood nearly in the middle of the room, her little body trembling under the shock of passions too strong for it, her very lips pale, and her eyes gleaming, the door opened, and Miss Assher appeared, tall, blooming, and splendid, in her walking costume. As she entered, her face wore the smile appropriate to the exits and entrances of a young lady who feels that her presence is an interesting fact, but the next moment she looked at Caterina with grave surprise, and then threw a glance of angry suspicion at Captain Wybrow, who wore an air of weariness and vexation.

'Perhaps you are too much engaged to walk out, Captain Wybrow? I will go alone.'

'No, no, I am coming,' he answered, hurrying towards her, and leading her out of the room, leaving poor Caterina to feel all the reaction of shame and self-reproach after her outburst of passion.

## 12

'Pray, what is likely to be the next scene in the drama between you and Miss Sarti?' said Miss Assher to Captain Wybrow as soon as they were out on the gravel. 'It would be agreeable to have some idea of what is coming.'

Captain Wybrow was silent. He felt out of humour, wearied, annoyed. There come moments when one almost determines never again to oppose anything but dead silence to an angry woman. 'Now then, confound it,' he said to himself, 'I'm going to be battered on the other flank.' He looked resolutely at the horizon, with something more like a frown on his face than Beatrice had ever seen there.

After a pause of two or three minutes, she continued in a still haughtier tone, 'I suppose you are aware, Captain Wybrow, that I expect an explanation of what I have just seen.'

'I have no explanation, my dear Beatrice,' he answered at last, making a strong effort over himself, 'except what I have already given you. I hoped you would never recur to the subject.'

'Your explanation, however, is very far from satisfactory. I can only say that the airs Miss Sarti thinks herself entitled to put on towards you are quite incompatible with your position as regards me. And her behaviour to me is most insulting. I shall certainly not stay in the house under such circumstances, and mamma must state the reasons to Sir Christopher.'

'Beatrice,' said Captain Wybrow, his irritation giving way to alarm, 'I beseech you to be patient, and exercise your good feelings in this affair. It is very painful, I know, but I am sure you would be grieved to injure poor Caterina – to bring down my uncle's anger upon her. Consider what a poor little dependent thing she is.'

'It is very adroit of you to make these evasions, but do not suppose that they deceive me. Miss Sarti would never dare to behave to you as she does, if you had not flirted with her, or made love to her. I suppose she considers your engagement to me a breach of faith to her. I am much obliged to you, certainly, for making me Miss Sarti's rival. You have told me a falsehood, Captain Wybrow.'

'Beatrice, I solemnly declare to you that Caterina is nothing more to me than a girl I naturally feel kindly to – as a favourite of my uncle's, and a nice little thing enough. I should be glad to see her married to Gilfil tomorrow; that's a good proof that I'm not in love with her, I should think. As to the past, I may have shown her little attentions, which she has exaggerated and misinterpreted. What man is not liable to that sort of thing?'

'But what can she found her behaviour on? What had she been saying to you this morning to make her tremble and turn pale in that way?'

'O, I don't know. I just said something about her behaving peevishly. With that Italian blood of hers, there's no knowing how she may take what one says. She's a fierce little thing, though she seems so quiet generally.'

'But she ought to be made to know how unbecoming and indelicate her conduct is. For my part, I wonder Lady Cheverel has not noticed her short answers and the airs she puts on.'

'Let me beg of you, Beatrice, not to hint anything of the kind to Lady Cheverel. You must have observed how strict my aunt is. It never enters her head that a girl can be in love with a man who has not made her an offer.'

'Well, I shall let Miss Sarti know myself that I have observed her conduct. It will be only a charity to her.'

'Nay, dear, that will be doing nothing but harm. Caterina's temper is peculiar. The best thing you can do will be to leave her to herself as much as possible. It will all wear off. I've no doubt she'll be married to

Gilfil before long. Girls' fancies are easily diverted from one object to another. By jove, what a rate my heart is galloping at! These confounded palpitations get worse instead of better.'

Thus ended the conversation, so far as it concerned Caterina, not without leaving a distinct resolution in Captain Wybrow's mind – a resolution carried into effect the next day, when he was in the library with Sir Christopher for the purpose of discussing some arrangements about the approaching marriage.

'By the by,' he said carelessly, when the business came to a pause, and he was sauntering round the room with his hands in his coat-pockets, surveying the backs of the books that lined the walls, 'when is the wedding between Gilfil and Caterina to come off, sir? I've a fellow-feeling for a poor devil so many fathoms deep in love as Maynard. Why shouldn't their marriage happen as soon as ours? I suppose he has come to an understanding with Tina?'

'Why,' said Sir Christopher, 'I did think of letting the thing be until old Crichley died; he can't hold out very long, poor fellow; and then Maynard might have entered into matrimony and the rectory both at once. But, after all, that really is no good reason for waiting. There is no need for them to leave the Manor when they are married. The little monkey is quite old enough. It would be pretty to see her a matron, with a baby about the size of a kitten in her arms.'

'I think that system of waiting is always bad. And if I can further any settlement you would like to make on Caterina, I shall be delighted to carry out your wishes.'

'My dear boy, that's very good of you, but Maynard will have enough, and from what I know of him – and I know him well – I think he would rather provide for Caterina himself. However, now you have put this matter into my head, I begin to blame myself for not having thought of it before. I've been so wrapped up in Beatrice and you, you rascal, that I had really forgotten poor Maynard. And he's older than you – it's high time he was settled in life as a family man.'

Sir Christopher paused, took snuff in a meditative manner, and presently said, more to himself than to Anthony, who was humming a tune at the far end of the room, 'Yes, yes. It will be a capital plan to finish off all our family business at once.'

Riding out with Miss Assher the same morning, Captain Wybrow mentioned to her incidentally, that Sir Christopher was anxious to bring about the wedding between Gilfil and Caterina as soon as possible, and that he, for his part, should do all he could to further the affair. It would be the best thing in the world for Tina, in whose welfare he was really interested.

With Sir Christopher there was never any long interval between purpose and execution. He made up his mind promptly, and he acted promptly. On rising from luncheon, he said to Mr Gilfil, 'Come with me into the library, Maynard. I want to have a word with you.'

'Maynard, my boy,' he began, as soon as they were seated, tapping his snuffbox, and looking radiant at the idea of the unexpected pleasure he was about to give, 'why shouldn't we have two happy couples instead of one, before the autumn is over, eh?'

'Eh?' he repeated, after a moment's pause, lengthening out the monosyllable, taking a slow pinch, and looking up at Maynard with a sly smile.

'I'm not quite sure that I understand you, sir,' answered Mr Gilfil, who felt annoyed at the consciousness that he was turning pale.

'Not understand me, you rogue? You know very well whose happiness lies nearest to my heart after Anthony's. You know you let me into your secrets long ago, so there's no confession to make. Tina's quite old enough to be a grave little wife now, and though the rectory's not ready for you, that's no matter. My lady and I shall feel all the more comfortable for having you with us. We should miss our little singing-bird if we lost her all at once.'

Mr Gilfil felt himself in a painfully difficult position. He dreaded that Sir Christopher should surmise or discover the true state of Caterina's feelings, and yet he was obliged to make those feelings the ground of his reply.

'My dear sir,' he at last said with some effort, 'you will not suppose that I am not alive to your goodness – that I am not grateful for your fatherly interest in my happiness, but I fear that Caterina's feelings towards me are not such as to warrant the hope that she would accept a proposal of marriage from me.'

'Have you ever asked her?'

'No, sir. But we often know these things too well without asking.'

'Pooh, pooh! the little monkey *must* love you. Why, you were her first playfellow; and I remember she used to cry if you cut your finger. Besides, she has always silently admitted that you were her lover. You know I have always spoken of you to her in that light. I took it for granted you had settled the business between yourselves; so did Anthony. Anthony thinks she's in love with you, and he has young eyes, which are apt enough to see clearly in these matters. He was talking to me about it this morning, and pleased me very much by the friendly interest he showed in you and Tina.'

The blood – more than was wanted – rushed back to Mr Gilfil's face; he set his teeth and clenched his hands in the effort to repress a burst of indignation. Sir Christopher noticed the flush, but thought it indicated the fluctuation of hope and fear about Caterina. He went on: 'You're too modest by half, Maynard. A fellow who can take a five-barred gate as you can, ought not to be so faint-hearted. If you can't speak to her yourself, leave me to talk to her.'

'Sir Christopher,' said poor Maynard earnestly, 'I shall really feel it the greatest kindness you can possibly show me not to mention this subject to Caterina at present. I think such a proposal, made pre-maturely, might only alienate her from me.'

Sir Christopher was getting a little displeased at this contradiction. His tone became a little sharper as he said, 'Have you any grounds to state for this opinion, beyond your general notion that Tina is not enough in love with you?'

'I can state none beyond my own very strong impression that she does not love me well enough to marry me.'

'Then I think that ground is worth nothing at all. I am tolerably correct in my judgement of people, and if I am not very much deceived in Tina, she looks forward to nothing else but to your being her husband. Leave me to manage the matter as I think best. You may rely on me that I shall do no harm to your cause, Maynard.'

Mr Gilfil, afraid to say more, yet wretched in the prospect of what might result from Sir Christopher's determination, quitted the library in a state of mingled indignation against Captain Wybrow, and distress for himself and Caterina. What would she think of him? She might suppose that *he* had instigated or sanctioned Sir Christopher's proceeding. He should perhaps not have an opportunity of speaking to her on the subject in time; he would write her a note, and carry it up to her room after the dressing-bell had rung. No; that would agitate her, and unfit her for appearing at dinner, and passing the evening calmly. He would defer it till bedtime. After prayers, he contrived to lead her back to the drawing room, and to put a letter in her hand. She carried it up to her own room, wondering, and there read –

*Dear Caterina,*

*Do not suspect for a moment that anything Sir Christopher may say to you about our marriage has been prompted by me. I have done all I dare do to dissuade him from urging the subject, and have only been prevented from speaking more strongly by the dread of provoking questions that I could not answer without causing you fresh misery. I write this, both to prepare you for anything Sir Christopher may say, and to assure you – but I hope you already believe it – that your feelings are sacred to me. I would rather part with the dearest hope of my life than be the means of adding to your trouble.*

*It is Captain Wybrow who has prompted Sir Christopher to take up the subject at this moment. I tell you this, to save you from hearing it suddenly when you are with Sir Christopher. You see now what sort of stuff that dastard's heart is made of. Trust in me always, dearest Caterina, as – whatever may come – your faithful friend and brother,*
*– Maynard Gilfil.*

Caterina was at first too terribly stung by the words about Captain Wybrow to think of the difficulty that threatened her – to think either of what Sir Christopher would say to her, or of what she could say in reply. Bitter sense of injury, fierce resentment, left no room for fear. With the poisoned garment upon him, the victim writhes under the torture – he has no thought of the coming death.

Anthony could do this! – Of this there could be no explanation but the coolest contempt for her feelings, the basest sacrifice of all the consideration and tenderness he owed her to the ease of his position with Miss Assher. No. It was worse than that: it was deliberate, gratuitous cruelty. He wanted to show her how he despised her; he wanted to make her feel her folly in having ever believed that he loved her.

The last crystal drops of trust and tenderness, she thought, were dried up; all was parched, fiery hatred. Now she need no longer check her resentment by the fear of doing him an injustice: he *had* trifled with her, as Maynard had said; he *had* been reckless of her; and now he was base and cruel. She had cause enough for her bitterness and anger; they were not so wicked as they had seemed to her.

As these thoughts were hurrying after each other like so many sharp throbs of fevered pain, she shed no tear. She paced restlessly to and fro, as her habit was – her hands clenched, her eyes gleaming fiercely and wandering uneasily, as if in search of something on which she might throw herself like a tigress.

'If I could speak to him,' she whispered, 'and tell him I hate him, I despise him, I loathe him!'

Suddenly, as if a new thought had struck her, she drew a key from her pocket, and, unlocking an inlaid desk where she stored up her keep-sakes, took from it a small miniature. It was in a very slight gold frame, with a ring to it, as if intended to be worn on a chain, and under the glass at the back were two locks of hair, one dark and the other auburn, arranged in a fantastic knot. It was Anthony's secret present to her a year ago – a copy he had had made specially for her. For the last month she had not taken it from its hiding-place: there was no need to heighten the vividness of the past. But now she clutched it fiercely, and dashed it across the room against the bare hearthstone.

Will she crush it under her feet, and grind it under her high-heeled shoe, till every trace of those false cruel features is gone? Ah, no! She rushed across the room, but when she saw the little treasure she had cherished so fondly, so often smothered with kisses, so often laid under her pillow, and remembered with the first return of consciousness in the morning – when she saw this one visible relic of the too-happy past lying with the glass shivered, the hair fallen out, the thin ivory cracked, there was a revulsion of the overstrained feeling: relenting came, and she burst into tears.

Look at her stooping down to gather up her treasure, searching for the hair and replacing it, and then mournfully examining the crack that disfigures the once-loved image. Alas! there is no glass now to guard either the hair or the portrait, but see how carefully she wraps delicate paper round it, and locks it up again in its old place. Poor child! God send the relenting may always come before the worst irrevocable deed!

This action had quieted her, and she sat down to read Maynard's letter again. She read it two or three times without seeming to take in the sense; her apprehension was dulled by the passion of the last hour, and she found it difficult to call up the ideas suggested by the words. At last she began to have a distinct conception of the impending interview with Sir Christopher. The idea of displeasing the Baronet, of whom everyone at the Manor stood in awe, frightened her so much that she thought it would be impossible to resist his wish. He believed that she loved Maynard; he had always spoken as if he were quite sure of it. How could she tell him he was deceived – and what if he were to ask her whether she loved anybody else? To have Sir Christopher looking angrily at her was more than she could bear, even in imagination. He had always been so good to her! Then she began to think of the pain she might give him, and the more selfish distress of fear gave way to the distress of affection. Unselfish tears began to flow, and sorrowful gratitude to Sir Christopher helped to awaken her sensibility to Mr Gilfil's tenderness and generosity.

'Dear, good Maynard! – what a poor return I make him! If I could but have loved him instead – but I can never love or care for anything again. My heart is broken.'

*13*

The next morning the dreaded moment came. Caterina, stupified by the suffering of the previous night, with that dull mental aching that follows on acute anguish, was in Lady Cheverel's sitting room, copying out some charity lists, when her ladyship came in, and said, 'Tina, Sir Christopher wants you; go down into the library.'

She went down trembling. As soon as she entered, Sir Christopher, who was seated near his writing-table, said, 'Now, little monkey, come and sit down by me; I have something to tell you.'

Caterina took a footstool, and seated herself on it at the Baronet's feet. It was her habit to sit on these low stools, and in this way she could hide her face better. She put her little arm round his leg, and leaned her cheek against his knee.

'Why, you seem out of spirits this morning, Tina. What's the matter, eh?'

'Nothing, Padroncello; only my head is bad.'

'Poor monkey! Well, now, wouldn't it do the head good if I were to promise you a good husband, and smart little wedding-gowns, and by and by a house of your own, where you would be a little mistress, and Padroncello would come and see you sometimes?'

'O no, no! I shouldn't like ever to be married. Let me always stay with you.'

'Pooh, pooh, little simpleton. I shall get old and tiresome, and there will be Anthony's children putting your nose out of joint. You will want someone to love you best of all, and you must have children of your own to love. I can't have you withering away into an old maid. I hate old maids: they make me dismal to look at them. I never see Sharp without shuddering. My little black-eyed monkey was never meant for anything so ugly. And there's Maynard Gilfil the best man in the county, worth his weight in gold, heavy as he is; he loves you better than his eyes. And you love him too, you silly monkey, whatever you may say about not being married.'

'No, no, dear Padroncello, do not say so; I could not marry him.'

'Why not, you foolish child? You don't know your own mind. Why, it is plain to everybody that you love him. My lady has all along said she was sure you loved him – she has seen what little princess airs you put on to him, and Anthony too, he thinks you are in love with Gilfil. Come, what has made you take it into your head that you wouldn't like to marry him?'

Caterina was now sobbing too deeply to make any answer. Sir Christopher patted her on the back and said, 'Come, come; why, Tina, you are not well this morning. Go and rest, little one. You will see things in quite another light when you are well. Think over what I have said, and remember there is nothing, after Anthony's marriage, that I have set my heart on so much as seeing you and Maynard settled for life. I must have no whims and follies – no nonsense.' This was said with a slight severity, but he presently added, in a soothing tone, 'There, there, stop crying, and be a good little monkey. Go and lie down and get to sleep.'

Caterina slipped from the stool on to her knees, took the old Baronet's hand, covered it with tears and kisses, and then ran out of the room.

Before the evening, Captain Wybrow had heard from his uncle the result of the interview with Caterina. He thought, 'If I could have a long quiet talk with her, I could perhaps persuade her to look more reasonably at things. But there's no speaking to her in the house without being interrupted, and I can hardly see her anywhere else without Beatrice's finding it out.' At last he determined to make it a matter of confidence with Miss Assher – to tell her that he wished to talk to Caterina quietly for the sake of bringing her to a calmer state of mind, and persuade her to listen to Gilfil's affection. He was very much pleased with this judicious and candid plan, and in the course of the evening he had arranged with himself the time and place of meeting, and had communicated his purpose to Miss Assher, who gave her entire approval. Anthony, she thought, would do well to speak plainly and seriously to Miss Sarti. He was really very patient and kind to her, considering how she behaved.

Tina had kept her room all that day, and had been carefully tended as an invalid, Sir Christopher having told her ladyship how matters stood. This tendance was so irksome to Caterina, she felt so uneasy under attentions and kindness that were based on a misconception, that she exerted herself to appear at breakfast the next morning, and declared herself well, though head and heart were throbbing. To be confined in her own room was intolerable; it was wretched enough to be looked at and spoken to, but it was more wretched to be left alone. She was frightened at her own sensations: she was frightened at the imperious vividness with which pictures of the past and future thrust themselves on her imagination. And there was another feeling, too, which made her want to be downstairs and moving about. Perhaps she might have an opportunity of speaking to Captain Wybrow alone – of speaking those words of hatred and scorn that burned on her tongue. That opportunity offered itself in a very unexpected manner.

Lady Cheverel having sent Caterina out of the drawing room to fetch some patterns of embroidery from her sitting room, Captain Wybrow presently walked out after her, and met her as she was returning down stairs.

'Caterina,' he said, laying his hand on her arm as she was hurrying on without looking at him, 'will you meet me in the Rookery at twelve o'clock? I must speak to you, and we shall be in privacy there. I cannot speak to you in the house.'

To his surprise, there was a flash of pleasure across her face; she answered shortly and decidedly, 'Yes', then snatched her arm away from him, and passed down stairs.

Miss Assher was this morning busy winding silks, being bent on emulating Lady Cheverel's embroidery, and Lady Assher chose the passive amusement of holding the skeins. Lady Cheverel had now all her working apparatus about her, and Caterina, thinking she was not wanted, went away and sat down to the harpsichord in the sitting room. It seemed as if playing massive chords – bringing out volumes of sound, would be the easiest way of passing the long feverish moments before twelve o'clock. Handel's *Messiah* stood open on the desk, at the chorus 'All we like sheep', and Caterina threw herself at once into the impetuous intricacies of that magnificent fugue. In her happiest moments she could never have played it so well: for now all the passion that made her misery was hurled by a convulsive effort into her music, just as pain gives new force to the clutch of the sinking wrestler, and as terror gives farsounding intensity to the shriek of the feeble.

But at half past eleven she was interrupted by Lady Cheverel, who said, 'Tina, go down, will you, and hold Miss Assher's silks for her. Lady Assher and I have decided on having our drive before luncheon.'

Caterina went down, wondering how she should escape from the drawing room in time to be in the Rookery at twelve. Nothing should prevent her from going; nothing should rob her of this one precious moment – perhaps the last – when she could speak out the thoughts that were in her. After that, she would be passive; she would bear anything.

But she had scarcely sat down with a skein of yellow silk on her hands, when Miss Assher said, graciously, 'I know you have an engagement with Captain Wybrow this morning. You must not let me detain you beyond the time.'

'So he has been talking to her about me,' thought Caterina. Her hands began to tremble as she held the skein.

Miss Assher continued in the same gracious tone: 'It is tedious work holding these skeins. I am sure I am very much obliged to you.'

'No, you are not obliged to me,' said Caterina, completely mastered by her irritation; 'I have only done it because Lady Cheverel told me.'

The moment was come when Miss Assher could no longer suppress her long latent desire to 'let Miss Sarti know the impropriety of her conduct'. With the malicious anger that assumes the tone of compassion, she said, 'Miss Sarti, I am really sorry for you, that you are not able to control yourself better. This giving way to unwarrantable feelings is lowering you – it is indeed.'

'What unwarrantable feelings?' said Caterina, letting her hands fall, and fixing her great dark eyes steadily on Miss Assher.

'It is quite unnecessary for me to say more. You must be conscious what I mean. Only summon a sense of duty to your aid. You are paining Captain Wybrow extremely by your want of self-control.'

'Did he tell you I pained him?'

'Yes, indeed, he did. He is very much hurt that you should behave to me as if you had a sort of enmity towards me. He would like you to make a friend of me. I assure you we both feel very kindly towards you, and are sorry you should cherish such feelings.'

'He is very good,' said Caterina, bitterly. 'What feelings did he say I cherished?'

This bitter tone increased Miss Assher's irritation. There was still a lurking suspicion in her mind, though she would not admit it to herself, that Captain Wybrow had told her a falsehood about his conduct and feelings towards Caterina. It was this suspicion, more even than the anger of the moment, which urged her to say something that would test the truth of his statement. That she would be humiliating Caterina at the same time was only an additional temptation.

'These are things I do not like to talk of, Miss Sarti. I cannot even understand how a woman can indulge a passion for a man who has never given her the least ground for it, as Captain Wybrow assures me is the case.'

'He told you that, did he?' said Caterina, in clear low tones, her lips turning white as she rose from her chair.

'Yes, indeed, he did. He was bound to tell it me after your strange behaviour.'

Caterina said nothing, but turned round suddenly and left the room.

See how she rushes noiselessly, like a pale meteor, along the passages and up the gallery stairs! Those gleaming eyes, those bloodless lips, that swift silent tread, make her look like the incarnation of a fierce purpose, rather than a woman. The midday sun is shining on the armour in the gallery, making mimic suns on bossed sword-hilts and the angles of polished breastplates. Yes, there are sharp weapons in the gallery. There is a dagger in that cabinet; she knows it well. And as a dragonfly wheels in its flight to alight for an instant on a leaf, she darts to the cabinet, takes out the dagger, and thrusts it into her pocket. In three minutes more she is out, in hat and cloak, on the gravel walk, hurrying along towards the thick shades of the distant Rookery. She threads the windings of the plantations, not feeling the golden leaves that rain upon her, not feeling the earth beneath her feet. Her hand is in her pocket, clenching the handle of the dagger, which she holds half out of its sheath.

She has reached the Rookery, and is under the gloom of the inter-lacing boughs. Her heart throbs as if it would burst her bosom – as if every next leap must be its last. Wait, wait, O heart! – till she has done this one deed. He will be there – he will be before her in a moment. He will come towards her with that false smile, thinking she does not know his baseness – she will plunge that dagger into his heart.

Poor child! poor child! she who used to cry to have the fish put back into the water – who never willingly killed the smallest living thing – dreams now, in the madness of her passion, that she can kill the man whose very voice unnerves her.

But what is that lying among the dank leaves on the path three yards before her?

Good God! it is he – lying motionless – his hat fallen off. He is ill, then – he has fainted. Her hand lets go the dagger, and she rushes towards him. His eyes are fixed; he does not see her. She sinks down on her knees, takes the dear head in her arms, and kisses the cold forehead.

'Anthony, Anthony! speak to me – it is Tina – speak to me! O God, he is dead!'

## 14

'Yes, Maynard,' said Sir Christopher, chatting with Mr Gilfil in the library, 'it really is a remarkable thing that I never in my life laid a plan, and failed to carry it out. I lay my plans well, and I never swerve from them – that's it. A strong will is the only magic. And next to striking out one's plans, the pleasantest thing in the world is to see them well accomplished. This year, now, will be the happiest of my life, all but the year '53, when I came into possession of the Manor, and married Henrietta. The last touch is given to the old house; Anthony's marriage – the thing I had nearest my heart – is settled to my entire satisfaction; and by and by you will be buying a little wedding ring for Tina's finger. Don't shake your head in that forlorn way; when I make prophecies they generally come to pass. But there's a quarter after twelve striking. I must be riding to the High Ash to meet Markham about felling some timber. My old oaks will have to groan for this wedding, but – '

The door burst open, and Caterina, ghastly and panting, her eyes distended with terror, rushed in, threw her arms round Sir Christopher's neck, and gasping out – 'Anthony... the Rookery... dead... in the Rookery', fell fainting on the floor.

In a moment Sir Christopher was out of the room, and Mr Gilfil was bending to raise Caterina in his arms. As he lifted her from the ground he felt something hard and heavy in her pocket. What could it be? The weight of it would be enough to hurt her as she lay. He carried her to the sofa, put his hand in her pocket, and drew forth the dagger.

Maynard shuddered. Did she mean to kill herself, then, or... or.. a horrible suspicion forced itself upon him. 'Dead – in the Rookery He hated himself for the thought that prompted him to draw the dagger from its sheath. No! there was no trace of blood, and he was ready to kiss the good steel for its innocence. He thrust the weapon into his own pocket; he would restore it as soon as possible to its well known place in the gallery. Yet, why had Caterina taken this dagger

What was it that had happened in the Rookery? Was it only a delirious vision of hers?

He was afraid to ring – afraid to summon anyone to Caterina's assistance. What might she not say when she awoke from this fainting fit? She might be raving. He could not leave her, and yet he felt as if he were guilty for not following Sir Christopher to see what was the truth. It took but a moment to think and feel all this, but that moment seemed such a long agony to him that he began to reproach himself for letting it pass without seeking some means of reviving Caterina. Happily the decanter of water on Sir Christopher's table was untouched. He would at least try the effect of throwing that water over her. She might revive without his needing to call anyone else.

Meanwhile Sir Christopher was hurrying at his utmost speed towards the Rookery; his face, so lately bright and confident, now agitated by a vague dread. The deep alarmed bark of Rupert, who ran by his side, had struck the ear of Mr Bates, then on his way homeward, as something un-wonted, and, hastening in the direction of the sound, he met the Baronet just as he was approaching the entrance of the Rookery. Sir Christopher's look was enough. Mr Bates said nothing, but hurried along by his side, while Rupert dashed forward among the dead leaves with his nose to the ground. They had scarcely lost sight of him a minute when a change in the tone of his bark told them that he had found something, and in an-other instant he was leaping back over one of the large planted mounds. They turned aside to ascend the mound, Rupert leading them; the tumultuous cawing of the rooks, the very rustling of the leaves, as their feet plunged among them, falling like an evil omen on the Baronet's ear.

They had reached the summit of the mound, and had begun to descend. Sir Christopher saw something purple down on the path below among the yellow leaves. Rupert was already beside it, but Sir Christopher could not move faster. A tremor had taken hold of the firm limbs. Rupert came back and licked the trembling hand, as if to say 'Courage!' and then was down again snuffing the body. Yes, it was a body... Anthony's body. There was the white hand with its diamond ring clutching the dark leaves. His eyes were half open, but did not heed the gleam of sunlight that darted itself directly on them from between the boughs.

Still he might only have fainted; it might only be a fit. Sir Christopher knelt down, unfastened the cravat, unfastened the waistcoat, and laid his hand on the heart. It might be syncope; it might not – it could not be death. No! that thought must be kept far off.

'Go, Bates, get help; we'll carry him to your cottage. Send someone to the house to tell Mr Gilfil and Warren. Bid them send off for Doctor Hart, and break it to my lady and Miss Assher that Anthony is ill.'

Mr Bates hastened away, and the Baronet was left alone kneeling beside the body. The young and supple limbs, the rounded cheeks, the delicate ripe lips, the smooth white hands, were lying cold and rigid, and the aged face was bending over them in silent anguish; the aged deep-veined hands were seeking with tremulous enquiring touches for some symptom that life was not irrevocably gone.

Rupert was there too, waiting and watching; licking first the dead and then the living hands; then running off on Mr Bates's track as if he would follow and hasten his return, but in a moment turning back again, unable to quit the scene of his master's sorrow.

15

It is a wonderful moment, the first time we stand by one who has fainted, and witness the fresh birth of consciousness spreading itself over the blank features, like the rising sunlight on the alpine summits that lay ghastly and dead under the leaden twilight. A slight shudder, and the frost-bound eyes recover their liquid light; for an instant they show the inward semi-consciousness of an infant's; then, with a little start, they open wider and begin to look; the present is visible, but only as a strange writing, and the interpreter Memory is not yet there.

Mr Gilfil felt a trembling joy as this change passed over Caterina's face. He bent over her, rubbing her chill hands, and looking at her with tender pity as her dark eyes opened on him wonderingly. He thought there might be some wine in the dining room close by. He left the room, and Caterina's eyes turned towards the window – towards Sir Christopher's chair. There was the link at which the chain of consciousness had snapped, and the events of the morning were beginning

94

to recur dimly like a half-remembered dream, when Maynard returned with some wine. He raised her, and she drank it, but still she was silent, seeming lost in the attempt to recover the past, when the door opened, and Mr Warren appeared with looks that announced terrible tidings. Mr Gilfil, dreading lest he should tell them in Caterina's presence, hurried towards him with his finger on his lips, and drew him away into the dining room on the opposite side of the passage.

Caterina, revived by the stimulant, was now recovering the full consciousness of the scene in the Rookery. Anthony was lying there dead; she had left him to tell Sir Christopher; she must go and see what they were doing with him; perhaps he was not really dead – only in a trance; people did fall into trances sometimes. While Mr Gilfil was telling Warren how it would be best to break the news to Lady Cheverel and Miss Assher, anxious himself to return to Caterina, the poor child had made her way feebly to the great entrance-door, which stood open. Her strength increased as she moved and breathed the fresh air, and with every increase of strength came increased vividness of emotion, increased yearning to be where her thought was – in the Rookery with Anthony. She walked more and more swiftly, and at last, gathering the artificial strength of passionate excitement, began to run.

But now she heard the tread of heavy steps, and under the yellow shade near the wooden bridge she saw men slowly carrying something. Soon she was face to face with them. Anthony was no longer in the Rookery: they were carrying him stretched on a door, and there behind him was Sir Christopher, with the firmly set mouth, the deathly pale-ness, and the concentrated expression of suffering in the eye, which mark the suppressed grief of the strong man. The sight of this face, on which Caterina had never before beheld the signs of anguish, caused a rush of new feeling that for the moment submerged all the rest. She went gently up to him, put her little hand in his, and walked in silence by his side. Sir Christopher could not tell her to leave him, and so she went on with that sad procession to Mr Bates's cottage in the Mosslands, and sat there in silence, waiting and watching to know if Anthony were really dead. She had not yet missed the dagger from her pocket; she had not yet even thought of it. At the sight of Anthony lying dead, her nature had rebounded from its new bias of resentment and hatred to the old sweet habit of love. The earliest and the longest has still the mastery over us, and the only past that linked itself with those glazed unconscious eyes was the past when they beamed on her with tenderness. She forgot the interval of wrong and jealousy and hatred – all his cruelty, and all her thoughts of revenge – as the exile forgets the stormy passage that lay between home and happiness and the dreary land in which he finds himself desolate.

## 16

Before night all hope was gone. Dr Hart had said it was death; Anthony's body had been carried to the house, and everyone there knew the calamity that had fallen on them.

Caterina had been questioned by Dr Hart, and had answered briefly that she found Anthony lying in the Rookery. That she should have been walking there just at that time was not a coincidence to raise conjectures in anyone besides Mr Gilfil. Except in answering this question, she had not broken her silence. She sat mute in a corner of the gardener's kitchen shaking her head when Maynard entreated her to return with him, and apparently unable to think of anything but the possibility that Anthony might revive, until she saw them carrying away the body to the house. Then she followed by Sir Christopher's side again, so quietly, that even Dr Hart did not object to her presence.

It was decided to lay the body in the library until after the coroner's inquest tomorrow, and when Caterina saw the door finally closed, she turned up the gallery stairs on her way to her own room, the place where she felt at home with her sorrows. It was the first time she had been in the gallery since that terrible moment in the morning, and now the spot and the objects around began to reawaken her half-stunned memory. The armour was no longer glittering in the sunlight, but there it hung dead and sombre above the cabinet from which she had taken the dagger. Yes! now it all came back to her – all the wretchedness and all the sin. But where was the dagger now? She felt in her pocket; it was not there. Could it have been her fancy – all that about the dagger? She looked in the cabinet; it was not there. Alas! no; it could not have been her fancy, and she *was* guilty of that wickedness. But where could the dagger be now? Could it have fallen out of her pocket? She heard steps ascending the stairs, and hurried on to her room, where, kneeling by the bed, and burying her face to shut out the hateful light, she tried to recall every feeling and incident of the morning.

It all came back; everything Anthony had done, and everything she had felt for the last month – for many months – ever since that June evening when he had last spoken to her in the gallery. She looked back on her storms of passion, her jealousy and hatred of Miss Assher, her thoughts of revenge on Anthony. O how wicked she had been! It was she who had been sinning; it was she who had driven him to do and say those things that had made her so angry. And if he had wronged her, what had she been on the verge of doing to him? She was too wicked ever to be pardoned. She would like to confess how wicked she had been, that they might punish her; she would like to humble herself to the dust before everyone – before Miss Assher even. Sir Christopher would send her away – would never see her again, if he knew all, and she would be happier to be punished and frowned on, than to be treated tenderly while she had that guilty secret in her breast. But then, if Sir Christopher were to know all, it would add to his sorrow, and make him more wretched than ever. No! she could not confess it – she should have to tell about Anthony. But she could not stay at the Manor; she must go away; she could not bear Sir Christopher's eye, could not bear the sight of all these things that reminded her of Anthony and of her sin. Perhaps she should die soon: she felt very feeble; there could not be much life in her. She would go away and live humbly, and pray to God to pardon her, and let her die.

The poor child never thought of suicide. No sooner was the storm of anger passed than the tenderness and timidity of her nature returned, and she could do nothing but love and mourn. Her inexperience prevented her from imagining the consequences of her disappearance from the Manor; she foresaw none of the terrible details of alarm and distress and search that must ensue. 'They will think I am dead,' she said to herself, 'and by and by they will forget me, and Maynard will get happy again, and love someone else.'

She was roused from her absorption by a knock at the door. Mrs Bellamy was there. She had come by Mr Gilfil's request to see how Miss Sarti was, and to bring her some food and wine.

'You look sadly, my dear,' said the old housekeeper, 'an' you're all of a quake wi' cold. Get you to bed, now do. Martha shall come an' warm it, an' light your fire. See now, here's some nice arrowroot, wi' a drop o' wine in it. Take that, an' it'll warm you. I must go down again, for I can't awhile to stay. There's so many things to see to; an' Miss Assher's in hysterics constant, an' her maid's ill i' bed – a poor creachy[33] thing – an' Mrs Sharp's wanted every minute. But I'll send Martha up, an' do you get ready to go to bed, there's a dear child, an' take care o' yourself.'

'Thank you, dear mammy,' said Tina, kissing the little old woman's wrinkled cheek; 'I shall eat the arrowroot, and don't trouble about me any more tonight. I shall do very well when Martha has lighted my fire. Tell Mr Gilfil I'm better. I shall go to bed by and by, so don't you come up again, because you may only disturb me.'

'Well, well, take care o' yourself, there's a good child, an' God send you may sleep.'

Caterina took the arrowroot quite eagerly, while Martha was lighting her fire. She wanted to get strength for her journey, and she kept the plate of biscuits by her that she might put some in her pocket. Her whole mind was now bent on going away from the Manor, and she was thinking of all the ways and means her little life's experience could suggest.

It was dusk now; she must wait till early dawn, for she was too timid to go away in the dark, but she must make her escape before anyone was up in the house. There would be people watching Anthony in the library, but she could make her way out of a small door leading into the garden, against the drawing room on the other side of the house.

She laid her cloak, bonnet, and veil ready; then she lighted a candle, opened her desk, and took out the broken portrait wrapped in paper. She folded it again in two little notes of Anthony's, written in pencil, and placed it in her bosom. There was the little china box, too – Dorcas' present, the pearl earrings, and a silk purse, with fifteen seven-shilling pieces in it, the presents Sir Christopher had made her on her birthday, ever since she had been at the Manor. Should she take the earrings and the seven-shilling pieces? She could not bear to part with them; it seemed as if they had some of Sir Christopher's love in them. She would like them to be buried with her. She fastened the little round earrings in her ears, and put the purse with Dorcas' box in her pocket. She had another purse there, and she took it out to count her money, for she would never spend her seven-shilling pieces. She had a guinea and eight shillings; that would be plenty.

So now she sat down to wait for the morning, afraid to lay herself on the bed lest she should sleep too long. If she could but see Anthony once more and kiss his cold forehead! But that could not be. She did not deserve it. She must go away from him, away from Sir Christopher, and Lady Cheverel, and Maynard, and everybody who had been kind to her, and thought her good while she was so wicked.

### 17

Some of Mrs Sharp's earliest thoughts, the next morning, were given to Caterina whom she had not been able to visit the evening before, and whom, from a nearly equal mixture of affection and self-importance, she did not at all like resigning to Mrs Bellamy's care. At half past eight o'clock she went up to Tina's room, bent on benevolent dictation as to doses and diet and lying in bed. But on opening the door she found the bed smooth and empty. Evidently it had not been slept in. What could this mean? Had she sat up all night, and was she gone out to walk? The poor thing's head might be touched by what had happened yesterday; it was such a shock – finding Captain Wybrow in that way; she was perhaps gone out of her mind. Mrs Sharp looked anxiously in the place where Tina kept her hat and cloak; they were not there, so that she had had at least the presence of mind to put them on. Still the good woman felt greatly alarmed, and hastened away to tell Mr Gilfil, who, she knew, was in his study.

'Mr Gilfil,' she said, as soon as she had closed the door behind her, 'my mind misgives me dreadful about Miss Sarti.'

'What is it?' said poor Maynard, with a horrible fear that Caterina had betrayed something about the dagger.

'She's not in her room, an' her bed's not been slept in this night, an' her hat an' cloak's gone.'

For a minute or two Mr Gilfil was unable to speak. He felt sure the worst had come: Caterina had destroyed herself. The strong man suddenly looked so ill and helpless that Mrs Sharp began to be frightened at the effect of her abruptness.

'O, sir, I'm grieved to my heart to shock you so, but I didn't know who else to go to.'

'No, no, you were quite right.'

He gathered some strength from his very despair. It was all over, and he had nothing now to do but to suffer and to help the suffering. He went on in a firmer voice – 'Be sure not to breathe a word about it to anyone. We must not alarm Lady Cheverel and Sir Christopher. Miss Sarti may be only walking in the garden. She was terribly excited by what she saw yesterday, and perhaps was unable to lie down from restlessness. Just go quietly through the empty rooms, and see whether she is in the house. I will go and look for her in the grounds.'

He went down, and, to avoid giving any alarm in the house, walked at once towards the Mosslands in search of Mr Bates, whom he met returning from his breakfast. To the gardener he confided his fear about Caterina, assigning as a reason for this fear the probability that the shock she had undergone yesterday had unhinged her mind, and begging him to send men in search of her through the gardens and park, and enquire if she had been seen at the lodges, and if she were not found or heard of in this way, to lose no time in dragging the waters round the Manor.

'God forbid it should be so, Bates, but we shall be the easier for having searched everywhere.'

'Troost to mae, troost to mae, Mr Gilfil. Eh! but I'd ha' worked for day-wage all the rest o' my life, rether than anythin' should ha' happened to her.'

The good gardener, in deep distress, strode away to the stables that he might send the grooms on horseback through the park.

Mr Gilfil's next thought was to search the Rookery: she might be haunting the scene of Captain Wybrow's death. He went hastily over every mound, looked round every large tree, and followed every winding of the walks. In reality he had little hope of finding her there; but the bare possibility fenced off for a time the fatal conviction that Caterina's body would be found in the water. When the Rookery had been searched in vain, he walked fast to the border of the little stream that bounded one side of the grounds. The stream was almost everywhere hidden among trees, and there was one place where it was broader and deeper than elsewhere – she would be more likely to come to that spot than to the pool. He hurried along with strained eyes, his imagination continually creating what he dreaded to see.

There is something white behind that overhanging bough. His knees tremble under him. He seems to see part of her dress caught on a branch, and her dear dead face upturned. O God, give strength to thy creature, on whom thou hast laid this great agony! He is nearly up to the bough, and the white object is moving. It is a waterfowl, that spreads its wings and flies away screaming. He hardly knows whether it is a relief or a disappointment that she is not there. The conviction that she is dead presses its cold weight upon him none the less heavily.

As he reached the great pool in front of the Manor, he saw Mr Bates, with a group of men already there, preparing for the dreadful search that could only displace his vague despair by a definite horror, for the gardener, in his restless anxiety, had been unable to defer this until other means of search had proved vain. The pool was not now laughing with sparkles among the water lilies. It looked black and cruel under the sombre sky, as if its cold depths held relentlessly all the murdered hope and joy of Maynard Gilfil's life.

Thoughts of the sad consequences for others as well as himself were crowding on his mind. The blinds and shutters were all closed in front of the Manor, and it was not likely that Sir Christopher would be aware of anything that was passing outside, but Mr Gilfil felt that Caterina's disappearance could not long be concealed from him. The coroner's inquest would be held shortly; she would be enquired for, and then it would be inevitable that the Baronet should know all.

At twelve o'clock, when all search and enquiry had been in vain, and the coroner was expected every moment, Mr Gilfil could no longer defer the hard duty of revealing this fresh calamity to Sir Christopher, who must otherwise have it discovered to him abruptly.

The Baronet was seated in his dressing room, where the dark window-curtains were drawn so as to admit only a sombre light. It was the first time Mr Gilfil had had an interview with him this morning, and he was struck to see how a single day and night of grief had aged the fine old man. The lines in his brow and about his mouth were deepened; his complexion looked dull and withered; there was a swollen ridge under his eyes; and the eyes themselves, which used to cast so keen a glance on the present, had the vacant expression that tells that vision is no longer a sense, but a memory.

He held out his hand to Maynard, who pressed it, and sat down beside him in silence. Sir Christopher's heart began to swell at this unspoken sympathy; the tears would rise, would roll in great drops down his cheeks. The first tears he had shed since boyhood were for Anthony.

Maynard felt as if his tongue were glued to the roof of his mouth. He could not speak first: he must wait until Sir Christopher said something which might lead on to the cruel words that must be spoken.

At last the Baronet mastered himself enough to say, 'I'm very weak, Maynard – God help me! I didn't think anything would unman me in this way; but I'd built everything on that lad. Perhaps I've been wrong in not forgiving my sister. She lost one of *her* sons a little while ago. I've been too proud and obstinate.'

'We can hardly learn humility and tenderness enough except by suffering,' said Maynard; 'and God sees we are in need of suffering, for it is falling more and more heavily on us. We have a new trouble this morning.'

'Tina?' said Sir Christopher, looking up anxiously – 'is Tina ill?'

'I am in dreadful uncertainty about her. She was very much agitated yesterday – and with her delicate health – I am afraid to think what turn the agitation may have taken.'

'Is she delirious, poor dear little one?'

'God only knows how she is. We are unable to find her. When Mrs Sharp went up to her room this morning, it was empty. She had not been in bed. Her hat and cloak were gone. I have had search made for her everywhere – in the house and garden, in the park, and – in the water. No one has seen her since Martha went up to light her fire at seven o'clock in the evening.'

While Mr Gilfil was speaking, Sir Christopher's eyes, which were eagerly turned on him, recovered some of their old keenness, and some sudden painful emotion, as at a new thought, flitted rapidly across his already agitated face, like the shadow of a dark cloud over the waves. When the pause came, he laid his hand on Mr Gilfil's arm, and said in a lower voice, 'Maynard, did that poor thing love Anthony?'

'She did.'

Maynard hesitated after these words, struggling between his reluctance to inflict a yet deeper wound on Sir Christopher, and his determination that no injustice should be done to Caterina. Sir Christopher's eyes were still fixed on him in solemn enquiry, and his own sunk towards the ground, while he tried to find the words that would tell the truth least cruelly.

'You must not have any wrong thoughts about Tina,' he said at length. 'I must tell you now, for her sake, what nothing but this should ever have caused to pass my lips. Captain Wybrow won her affections by attentions that, in his position, he was bound not to show her. Before his marriage was talked of, he had behaved to her like a lover.'

Sir Christopher relaxed his hold of Maynard's arm, and looked away from him. He was silent for some minutes, evidently attempting to master himself, so as to be able to speak calmly.

'I must see Henrietta immediately,' he said at last, with something of his old sharp decision; 'she must know all; but we must keep it from everyone else as far as possible. My dear boy,' he continued in a kinder tone, 'the heaviest burthen has fallen on you. But we may find her yet; we must not despair: there has not been time enough for us to be certain. Poor dear little one! God help me! I thought I saw everything, and was stone-blind all the while.'

## 19

The sad slow week was gone by at last. At the coroner's inquest a verdict of sudden death had been pronounced. Dr Hart, acquainted with Captain Wybrow's previous state of health, had given his opinion that death had been imminent from long-established disease of the heart, though it had probably been accelerated by some unusual emotion. Miss Assher was the only person who positively knew the motive that had led Captain Wybrow to the Rookery, but she had not mentioned Caterina's name, and all painful details or enquiries were studiously kept from her. Mr Gilfil and Sir Christopher, however, knew enough to conjecture that the fatal agitation was due to an appointed meeting with Caterina.

All search and enquiry after her had been fruitless, and were the more likely to be so because they were carried on under the prepossession that she had committed suicide. No one noticed the absence of the trifles she had taken from her desk; no one knew of the likeness, or that she had hoarded her seven-shilling pieces, and it was not remarkable that she should have happened to be wearing the pearl earrings. She had left the house, they thought, taking nothing with her; it seemed impossible she could have gone far, and she must have been in a state of mental excitement, which made it too probable she had only gone to seek relief in death. The same places within three or four miles of the Manor were searched again and again – every pond, every ditch in the neighbourhood was examined.

Sometimes Maynard thought that death might have come on unsought, from cold and exhaustion, and not a day passed but he wandered through the neighbouring woods, turning up the heaps of dead leaves, as if it were possible her dear body could be hidden there. Then another horrible thought recurred, and before each night came he had been again through all the uninhabited rooms of the house, to satisfy himself once more that she was not hidden behind some cabinet, or door, or curtain – that he should not find her there with madness in her eyes, looking and looking, and yet not seeing him.

But at last those five long days and nights were at an end, the funeral was over, and the carriages were returning through the park. When they had set out, a heavy rain was falling, but now the clouds were breaking up, and a gleam of sunshine was sparkling among the dripping boughs under which they were passing. This gleam fell upon a man on horseback who was jogging slowly along, and whom Mr Gilfil recognised, in spite of diminished rotundity, as Daniel Knott, the coachman who had married the rosy-cheeked Dorcas ten years before.

Every new incident suggested the same thought to Mr Gilfil, and his eye no sooner fell on Knott than he said to himself 'Can he be come to tell us anything about Caterina?' Then he remembered that Caterina had been very fond of Dorcas, and that she always had some present ready to send her when Knott paid an occasional visit to the Manor. Could Tina have gone to Dorcas? But his heart sank again as he thought, very likely Knott had only come because he had heard of Captain Wybrow's death, and wanted to know how his old master had borne the blow.

As soon as the carriage reached the house, he went up to his study and walked about nervously, longing, but afraid, to go down and speak to Knott, lest his faint hope should be dissipated. Anyone looking at that face, usually so full of calm goodwill, would have seen that the last week's suffering had left deep traces. By day he had been riding or wandering incessantly, either searching for Caterina himself, or directing enquiries to be made by others. By night he had not known sleep – only intermittent dozing, in which he seemed to be finding Caterina dead, and woke up with a start from this unreal agony to the real anguish of believing that he should see her no more. The clear grey eyes looked sunken and restless, the full careless lips had a strange tension about them, and the brow, formerly so smooth and open, was contracted as if with pain. He had not lost the object of a few months' passion; he had lost the being who was bound up with his power of loving, as the brook we played by or the flowers we gathered in childhood are bound up with our sense of beauty. Love meant nothing for him but to love Caterina. For years, the thought of her had been present in everything, like the air and the light; and now she was gone, it seemed as if all pleasure had lost its vehicle: the sky, the earth, the daily ride, the daily talk might be there, but the loveliness and the joy that were in them had gone for ever.

Presently, as he still paced backwards and forwards, he heard steps along the corridor, and there was a knock at his door. His voice trembled as he said 'Come in', and the rush of renewed hope was hardly distinguishable from pain when he saw Warren enter with Daniel Knott behind him.

'Knott is come, sir, with news of Miss Sarti. I thought it best to bring him to you first.'

Mr Gilfil could not help going up to the old coachman and wringing his hand, but he was unable to speak, and only motioned to him to take a chair, while Warren left the room. He hung upon Daniel's moon-face, and listened to his small piping voice, with the same solemn yearning expectation with which he would have given ear to the most awful messenger from the land of shades.

'It war Dorkis, sir, would hev me come, but we knowed nothin' o' what's happened at the Manor. She's frightened out on her wits about Miss Sarti, an' she would hev me saddle Blackbird this mornin', an' leave the ploughin', to come an' let Sir Christifer an' my lady know. P'raps you've heared, sir, we don't keep the Cross Keys at Sloppeter now; a uncle o' mine died three 'ear ago, an' left me a leggicy. He was bailiff to Squire Ramble, as hed them there big farms on his hans, an' so we took a little farm o' forty acres or thereabouts, becos Dorkis didn't like the public when she got moithered wi' children. As pritty a place as iver you see, sir, wi' water at the back convenent for the cattle.'

'For God's sake,' said Maynard, 'tell me what it is about Miss Sarti. Don't stay to tell me anything else now.'

'Well, sir,' said Knott, rather frightened by the parson's vehemence, 'she come t' our house i' the carrier's cart o' Wednesday, when it was welly nine o'clock at night, and Dorkis run out, for she heared the cart stop, an' Miss Sarti throwed her arms roun' Dorkis' neck an' says, "Tek me in, Dorkis, tek me in," an' went off into a swoond, like. An' Dorkis calls out to me – "Dannel," she calls – an' I run out and carried the young miss in, an' she come roun' arter a hit, an' opened her eyes, and Dorkis got her to drink a spoonful o' rum-an'-water – we've got some capital rum as we brought from the Cross Keys, and Dorkis won't let nobody drink it. She says she keeps it for sickness, but for my part, I think it's a pity to drink good rum when your mouth's out o' taste; you may just as well hev doctor's stuff. However, Dorkis got her to bed, an' there she's lay iver sin', stoopid like, an' niver speaks, an' on'y teks little bits an' sups when Dorkis coaxes her. An' we begun to be frightened, and couldn't think what had made her come away from the Manor, and Dorkis was afeared there was summat wrong. So this mornin' she could hold no longer, an' would hev no nay but I must come an' see, an' so I've rode twenty mile upo' Blackbird, as thinks all the while he's a-ploughin', an' turns sharp roun', every thirty yards, as if he was at the end of a furrow. I've hed a sore time wi' him, I can tell you, sir.'

'God bless you, Knott, for coming!' said Mr Gilfil, wringing the old coachman's hand again. 'Now go down and have something and rest yourself. You will stay here tonight, and by and by I shall come to you to learn the nearest way to your house. I shall get ready to ride there immediately, when I have spoken to Sir Christopher.'

In an hour from that time Mr Gilfil was galloping on a stout mare towards the little muddy village of Callam, five miles beyond Sloppeter. Once more he saw some gladness in the afternoon sunlight; once more it was a pleasure to see the hedgerow trees flying past him, and to be conscious of a 'good seat' while his black Kitty bounded beneath him, and the air whistled to the rhythm of her pace. Caterina was not dead; he had found her; his love and tenderness and long-suffering seemed so strong, they must recall her to life and happiness.

After that week of despair, the rebound was so violent that it carried his hopes at once as far as the utmost mark they had ever reached. Caterina would come to love him at last; she would be his. They had been carried through all that dark and weary way that she might know the depth of his love. How he would cherish her – his little bird with the timid bright eye, and the sweet throat that trembled with love and music! She would nestle against him, and the poor little breast that had been so ruffled and bruised should be safe for ever more. In the love of a brave and faithful man there is always a strain of maternal tenderness; he gives out again those beams of protecting fondness that were shed on him as he lay on his mother's knee. It was twilight as he entered the village of Callam, and, asking a homeward-bound labourer the way to Daniel Knott's, learned that it was by the church, which showed its stumpy ivy-clad spire on a slight elevation of ground; a useful addition to the means of identifying that desirable homestead afforded by Daniel's description – 'the prittiest place iver you see' – though a small cow-yard full of excellent manure, and leading right up to the door, without any frivolous interruption from garden or railing, might perhaps have been enough to make that description unmistakably specific.

Mr Gilfil had no sooner reached the gate leading into the cow-yard than he was descried by a flaxen-haired lad of nine, prematurely invested with the *toga virilis*,[34] or smock-frock, who ran forward to let in the unusual visitor. In a moment Dorcas was at the door, the roses on her cheeks apparently all the redder for the three pair of cheeks that formed a group round her, and for the very fat baby who stared in her arms, and sucked a long crust with calm relish.

'Is it Mr Gilfil, sir?' said Dorcas, curtsying low as he made his way through the damp straw, after tying up his horse.

'Yes, Dorcas; I'm grown out of your knowledge. How is Miss Sarti?'

'Just for all the world the same, sir, as I suppose Dannel's told you, for I reckon you've come from the Manor, though you're come uncommon quick, to be sure.'

'Yes, he got to the Manor about one o'clock, and I set off as soon as I could. She's not worse, is she?'

'No change, sir, for better or wuss. Will you please to walk in, sir? She lies there takin' no notice o' nothin', no more nor a baby as is on'y a week old, an' looks at me as blank as if she didn't know me. O what can it be, Mr Gilfil? How come she to leave the Manor? How's his honour an' my lady?'

'In great trouble, Dorcas. Captain Wybrow, Sir Christopher's nephew, you know, has died suddenly. Miss Sarti found him lying dead, and I think the shock has affected her mind.'

'Eh, dear! that fine young gentlemen as was to be th' heir, as Danne told me about. I remember seein' him when he was a little un, a-visitin at the Manor. Well-a-day, what a grief to his honour and my lady. But that poor Miss Tina – an' she found him a-lyin' dead? O dear, O dear!'

Dorcas had led the way into the best kitchen, as charming a room as best kitchens used to be in farmhouses that had no parlours – the fire reflected in a bright row of pewter plates and dishes; the sand-scoured deal tables so clean you longed to stroke them; the salt-coffer in one chimney-corner, and a three-cornered chair in the other, the walls behind handsomely tapestried with flitches of bacon, and the ceiling ornamented with pendent hams.

'Sit ye down, sir – do,' said Dorcas, moving the three-cornered chair, 'an' let me get you somethin' after your long journey. Here, Becky, come an' tek the baby.'

Becky, a red-armed damsel, emerged from the adjoining back-kitchen, and possessed herself of baby, whose feelings or fat made him conveniently apathetic under the transference.

'What'll you please to tek, sir, as I can give you? I'll get you a rasher o' bacon i' no time, an' I've got some tea, or belike you'd tek a glass o' rum-an'-water. I know we've got nothin' as you're used t' eat and drink, but such as I hev, sir, I shall be proud to give you.'

'Thank you, Dorcas; I can't eat or drink anything. I'm not hungry or tired. Let us talk about Tina. Has she spoken at all?'

'Niver since the fust words. "Dear Dorkis," says she, "tek me in;" an' then went off into a faint, an' not a word has she spoken since. I get her t' eat little bits an' sups o' things, but she teks no notice o' nothin'. I've took up Bessie wi' me now an' then' – here Dorcas lifted to her lap a curly-headed little girl of three, who was twisting a corner of her mother's apron, and opening round eyes at the gentleman – 'folks'll tek notice o' children sometimes when they won't o' nothin' else. An' we gathered the autumn crocuses out o' th' orchard, and Bessie carried 'em up in her hand, an' put 'em on the bed. I knowed how fond Miss Tina was o' flowers an' them things, when she was a little un. But she looked at Bessie an' the flowers just the same as if she didn't see 'em. It cuts me to th' heart to look at them eyes o' hers; I think they're bigger nor iver, an' they look like my poor baby's as died, when it got so thin – O dear, its little hands you could see thro' 'em. But I've great hopes if she was to see you, sir, as come from the Manor, it might bring back her mind, like.'

Maynard had that hope too, but he felt cold mists of fear gathering round him after the few bright warm hours of joyful confidence that had passed since he first heard that Caterina was alive. The thought *would* urge itself upon him that her mind and body might never recover the strain that had been put upon them – that her delicate thread of life had already nearly spun itself out.

'Go now, Dorcas, and see how she is, but don't say anything about my being here. Perhaps it would be better for me to wait till daylight before I see her, and yet it would be very hard to pass another night in this way.'

Dorcas set down little Bessie, and went away. The three other children, including young Daniel in his smock-frock, were standing opposite to Mr Gilfil, watching him still more shyly now they were without their mother's countenance. He drew little Bessie towards him, and set her on his knee. She shook her yellow curls out of her eyes, and looked up at him as she said, 'Zoo tome to tee ze yady? Zoo mek her peak? What zoo do to her? Tiss her?'

'Do you like to be kissed, Bessie?'

'Det,' said Bessie, immediately ducking down her head very low, in resistance to the expected rejoinder.

'We've got two pups,' said young Daniel, emboldened by observing the gentleman's amenities towards Bessie. 'Shall I show 'em yer? One's got white spots.'

'Yes, let me see them.'

Daniel ran out, and presently reappeared with two blind puppies, eagerly followed by the mother, affectionate though mongrel, and an exciting scene was beginning when Dorcas returned and said, 'There's niver any difference in her hardly. I think you needn't wait, sir. She lies very still, as she al'ys does. I've put two candle i' the room, so as she may see you well. You'll please t' excuse the room, sir, an' the cap as she has on; it's one o' mine.'

Mr Gilfil nodded silently, and rose to follow her upstairs. They turned in at the first door, their footsteps making little noise on the plaster floor. The red-checkered linen curtains were drawn at the head of the bed, and Dorcas had placed the candles on this side of the room, so that the light might not fall oppressively on Caterina's eyes. When she had opened the door, Dorcas whispered, 'I'd better leave you, sir, I think?'

Mr Gilfil motioned assent, and advanced beyond the curtain. Caterina lay with her eyes turned the other way, and seemed unconscious that anyone had entered. Her eyes, as Dorcas had said, looked larger than ever, perhaps because her face was thinner and paler, and her hair quite gathered away under one of Dorcas' thick caps. The small hands, too, that lay listlessly on the outside of the bedclothes were thinner than ever. She looked younger than she really was, and anyone seeing the tiny face and hands for the first time might have thought they belonged to a little girl of twelve, who was being taken away from coming instead of past sorrow.

When Mr Gilfil advanced and stood opposite to her, the light fell full upon his face. A slight startled expression came over Caterina's eyes; she looked at him earnestly for a few moments, then lifted up her hand as if to beckon him to stoop down towards her, and whispered 'Maynard!'

He seated himself on the bed, and stooped down towards her. She whispered again – 'Maynard, did you see the dagger?'

He followed his first impulse in answering her, and it was a wise one.

'Yes,' he whispered, 'I found it in your pocket, and put it back again in the cabinet.'

He took her hand in his and held it gently, awaiting what she would say next. His heart swelled so with thankfulness that she had recognised him, he could hardly repress a sob. Gradually her eyes became softer and less intense in their gaze. The tears were slowly gathering, and presently some large hot drops rolled down her cheek. Then the flood-gates were opened, and the heart-easing stream gushed forth; deep sobs came, and for nearly an hour she lay without speaking, while the heavy icy pressure that withheld her misery from utterance was thus melting away. How precious these tears were to Maynard, who day after day had been shuddering at the continually recurring image of Tina with the dry scorching stare of insanity!

By degrees the sobs subsided, she began to breathe calmly, and lay quiet with her eyes shut. Patiently Maynard sat, not heeding the flight of the hours, not heeding the old clock that ticked loudly on the landing. But when it was nearly ten, Dorcas, impatiently anxious to know the result of Mr Gilfil's appearance, could not help stepping in on tiptoe. Without moving, he whispered in her ear to supply him with candles, see that the cow-boy had shaken down his mare, and go to bed – he would watch with Caterina – a great change had come over her.

Before long, Tina's lips began to move. 'Maynard,' she whispered again. He leaned towards her, and she went on.

'You know how wicked I am, then? You know what I meant to do with the dagger?'

'Did you mean to kill yourself, Tina?'

She shook her head slowly, and then was silent for a long while. At last, looking at him with solemn eyes, she whispered, 'To kill *him*.'

'Tina, my loved one, you would never have done it. God saw your whole heart; He knows you would never harm a living thing. He watches over His children, and will not let them do things they would pray with their whole hearts not to do. It was the angry thought of a moment, and He forgives you.'

She sank into silence again till it was nearly midnight. The weary enfeebled spirit seemed to be making its slow way with difficulty through the windings of thought, and when she began to whisper again, it was in reply to Maynard's words.

'But I had had such wicked feelings for a long while. I was so angry, and I hated Miss Assher so, and I didn't care what came to anybody, because I was so miserable myself. I was full of bad passions. No one else was ever so wicked.'

'Yes, Tina, many are just as wicked. I often have very wicked feelings, and am tempted to do wrong things, but then my body is stronger than yours, and I can hide my feelings and resist them better. They do not master me so. You have seen the little birds when they are very young and just begin to fly, how all their feathers are ruffled when they are frightened or angry; they have no power over themselves left, and might fall into a pit from mere fright. You were like one of those little birds. Your sorrow and suffering had taken such hold of you, you hardly knew what you did.'

He would not speak long, lest he should tire her, and oppress her with too many thoughts. Long pauses seemed needful for her before she could concentrate her feelings in short words.

'But when I meant to do it,' was the next thing she whispered, 'it was as bad as if I had done it.'

'No, my Tina,' answered Maynard slowly, waiting a little between each sentence; 'we mean to do wicked things that we never could do, just as we mean to do good or clever things that we never could do. Our thoughts are often worse than we are, just as they are often better than we are. And God sees us as we are altogether, not in separate feelings or actions, as our fellow men see us. We are always doing each other injustice, and thinking better or worse of each other than we deserve, because we only hear and see separate words and actions. We don't see each other's whole nature. But God sees that you could not have committed that crime.'

Caterina shook her head slowly, and was silent. After a while, 'I don't know,' she said; 'I seemed to see him coming towards me, just as he would really have looked, and I meant – I meant to do it.'

'But when you saw him – tell me how it was, Tina?'

'I saw him lying on the ground and thought he was ill. I don't know how it was then; I forgot everything. I knelt down and spoke to him, and – and he took no notice of me, and his eyes were fixed, and I began to think he was dead.'

'And you have never felt angry since?'

'O no, no; it is I who have been more wicked than anyone; it is I who have been wrong all through.'

'No, Tina; the fault has not all been yours; *he* was wrong; he gave you provocation. And wrong makes wrong. When people use us ill, we can hardly help having ill feeling towards them. But that second wrong is more excusable. I am more sinful than you, Tina; I have often had very bad feelings towards Captain Wybrow, and if he had provoked me as he did you, I should perhaps have done something more wicked.'

'O, it was not so wrong in him; he didn't know how he hurt me. How was it likely he could love me as I loved him? And how could he marry a poor little thing like me?'

Maynard made no reply to this, and there was again silence, till Tina said, 'Then I was so deceitful; they didn't know how wicked I was. Padroncello didn't know; his good little monkey he used to call me, and if he had known, O how naughty he would have thought me!'

'My Tina, we have all our secret sins, and if we knew ourselves, we should not judge each other harshly. Sir Christopher himself has felt, since this trouble came upon him, that he has been too severe and obstinate.'

In this way – in these broken confessions and answering words of comfort – the hours wore on, from the deep black night to the chill early twilight, and from early twilight to the first yellow streak of morning parting the purple cloud. Mr Gilfil felt as if in the long hours of that night the bond that united his love for ever and alone to Caterina had acquired fresh strength and sanctity. It is so with the human relations that rest on the deep emotional sympathy of affection: every new day and night of joy or sorrow is a new ground, a new consecration, for the love that is nourished by memories as well as hopes – the love to which perpetual repetition is not a weariness but a want, and to which a separated joy is the beginning of pain.

The cocks began to crow; the gate swung; there was a tramp of footsteps in the yard, and Mr Gilfil heard Dorcas stirring. These sounds seemed to affect Caterina, for she looked anxiously at him and said, 'Maynard, are you going away?'

'No, I shall stay here at Callam until you are better, and then you will go away too.'

'Never to the Manor again, O no! I shall live poorly, and get my own bread.'

'Well, dearest, you shall do what you would like best. But I wish you could go to sleep now. Try to rest quietly, and by and by you will perhaps sit up a little. God has kept you in life in spite of all this sorrow; it will be sinful not to try and make the best of His gift. Dear Tina, you will try – and little Bessie brought you some crocuses once, you didn't notice the poor little thing, but you *will* notice her when she comes again, will you not?'

'I will try,' whispered Tina humbly, and then closed her eyes.

By the time the sun was above the horizon, scattering the clouds, and shining with pleasant morning warmth through the little leaded window, Caterina was asleep. Maynard gently loosed the tiny hand, cheered Dorcas with the good news, and made his way to the village inn, with a thankful heart that Tina had been so far herself again. Evidently the sight of him had blended naturally with the memories in which her mind was absorbed, and she had been led on to an unburthening of herself that might be the beginning of a complete restoration. But her body was so enfeebled – her soul so bruised – that the utmost tenderness and care would be necessary. The next thing to be done was to send tidings to Sir Christopher and Lady Cheverel, then to write and summon his sister, under whose care he had determined to place Caterina. The Manor, even if she had been wishing to return thither, would, he knew, be the most undesirable home for her at present: every scene, every object there, was associated with still unallayed anguish. If she were domesticated for a time with his mild gentle sister, who had a peaceful home and a prattling little boy, Tina might attach herself anew to life, and recover, partly at least, the shock that had been given to her constitution. When he had written his letters and taken a hasty breakfast, he was soon in his saddle again, on his way to Sloppeter, where he would post them, and seek out a medical man, to whom he might confide the moral causes of Caterina's enfeebled condition.

## 20

In less than a week from that time, Caterina was persuaded to travel in a comfortable carriage, under the care of Mr Gilfil and his sister, Mrs Heron, whose soft blue eyes and mild manners were very soothing to the poor bruised child – the more so as they had an air of sisterly equality that was quite new to her. Under Lady Cheverel's uncaressing authoritative goodwill, Tina had always retained a certain constraint and awe, and there was a sweetness before unknown in having a young and gentle woman, like an elder sister, bending over her caressingly, and speaking in low loving tones.

Maynard was almost angry with himself for feeling happy while Tina's mind and body were still trembling on the verge of irrecoverable decline, but the new delight of acting as her guardian angel, of being with her every hour of the day, of devising everything for her comfort, of watching for a ray of returning interest in her eyes, was too absorbing to leave room for alarm or regret.

On the third day the carriage drove up to the door of Foxholm Parsonage, where the Revd Arthur Heron presented himself on the doorstep, eager to greet his returning Lucy, and holding by the hand a broad-chested tawny-haired boy of five, who was smacking a miniature hunting whip with great vigour.

Nowhere was there a lawn more smooth-shaven, walks better swept, or a porch more prettily festooned with creepers, than at Foxholm Parsonage, standing snugly sheltered by beeches and chestnuts halfway down the pretty green hill that was surmounted by the church, and overlooking a village that straggled at its ease among pastures and meadows, surrounded by wild hedgerows and broad shadowing trees, as yet unthreatened by improved methods of farming.

Brightly the fire shone in the great parlour, and brightly in the little pink bedroom, which was to be Caterina's, because it looked away from the churchyard, and on to a farm homestead, with its little cluster of beehive ricks, and placid groups of cows, and cheerful matin sounds of healthy labour. Mrs Heron, with the instinct of a delicate, impressible woman, had written to her husband to have this room prepared for Caterina. Contented speckled hens, industriously scratching for the rarely found corn, may sometimes do more for a sick heart than a grove of nightingales; there is something irresistibly calming in the unsentimental cheeriness of top-knotted pullets, unpetted sheepdogs, and patient carthorses enjoying a drink of muddy water.

In such a home as this parsonage, a nest of comfort, without any of the stateliness that would carry a suggestion of Cheverel Manor, Mr Gilfil was not unreasonable in hoping that Caterina might gradually shake off the haunting vision of the past, and recover from the languor and feebleness that were the physical sign of that vision's blighting presence. The next thing to be done was to arrange an exchange of duties with Mr Heron's curate, that Maynard might be constantly near Caterina, and watch over her progress. She seemed to like him to be with her, to look uneasily for his return, and though she seldom spoke to him, she was most contented when he sat by her, and held her tiny hand in his large protecting grasp. But Oswald, alias Ozzy, the broad-chested boy, was perhaps her most beneficial companion. With something of his uncle's person, he had inherited also his uncle's early taste for a domestic menagerie, and was very imperative in demanding Tina's sympathy in the welfare of his guinea pigs, squirrels, and dormice. With him she seemed now and then to have gleams of her childhood coming athwart the leaden clouds, and many hours of winter went by the more easily for being spent in Ozzy's nursery.

Mrs Heron was not musical, and had no instrument; but one of Mr Gilfil's cares was to procure a harpsichord, and have it placed in the drawing room, always open, in the hope that some day the spirit of music would be reawakened in Caterina, and she would be attracted towards the instrument. But the winter was almost gone by, and he had waited in vain. The utmost improvement in Tina had not gone beyond passiveness and acquiescence – a quiet grateful smile, compliance with Oswald's whims, and an increasing consciousness of what was being said and done around her. Sometimes she would take up a bit of woman's work, but she seemed too languid to persevere in it; her fingers soon dropped, and she relapsed into motionless reverie.

At last – it was one of those bright days in the end of February, when the sun is shining with a promise of approaching spring. Maynard had been walking with her and Oswald round the garden to look at the snowdrops, and she was resting on the sofa after the walk. Ozzy, roaming about the room in quest of a forbidden pleasure, came to the harpsichord, and struck the handle of his whip on a deep bass note.

The vibration rushed through Caterina like an electric shock: it seemed as if at that instant a new soul were entering into her, and filling her with a deeper, more significant life. She looked round, rose from the sofa, and walked to the harpsichord. In a moment her fingers were wandering with their old sweet method among the keys, and her soul was floating in its true familiar element of delicious sound, as the water-plant that lies withered and shrunken on the ground expands into freedom and beauty when once more bathed in its native flood.

Maynard thanked God. An active power was reawakened, and must make a new epoch in Caterina's recovery.

Presently there were low liquid notes blending themselves with the harder tones of the instrument, and gradually the pure voice swelled into predominance. Little Ozzy stood in the middle of the room, with his mouth open and his legs very wide apart, struck with something like awe at this new power in 'Tin-Tin,' as he called her, whom he had been accustomed to think of as a playfellow not at all clever, and very much in need of his instruction on many subjects. A genie soaring with broad wings out of his milk jug would not have been more astonishing.

Caterina was singing the very air from the *Orfeo* that we heard her singing so many months ago at the beginning of her sorrows. It was '*Ho perduto*', Sir Christopher's favourite, and its notes seemed to carry on their wings all the tenderest memories of her life, when Cheverel Manor was still an untroubled home. The long happy days of childhood and girlhood recovered all their rightful predominance over the short interval of sin and sorrow.

She paused, and burst into tears – the first tears she had shed since she had been at Foxholm. Maynard could not help hurrying towards her, putting his arm round her, and leaning down to kiss her hair. She nestled to him, and put up her little mouth to be kissed.

The delicate-tendrilled plant must have something to cling to. The soul that was born anew to music was born anew to love.

## 21

On the 30th of May 1790, a very pretty sight was seen by the villagers assembled near the door of Foxholm Church. The sun was bright upon the dewy grass, the air was alive with the murmur of bees and the trilling of birds, the bushy blossoming chestnuts and the foamy flower-ing hedgerows seemed to be crowding round to learn why the church bells were ringing so merrily, as Maynard Gilfil, his face bright with happiness, walked out of the old Gothic doorway with Tina on his arm. The little face was still pale, and there was a subdued melancholy in it, as of one who sups with friends for the last time, and has his ear open for the signal that will call him away. But the tiny hand rested with the pressure of contented affection on Maynard's arm, and the dark eyes met his downward glance with timid answering love.

There was no train of bridesmaids; only pretty Mrs Heron leaning on the arm of a dark-haired young man hitherto unknown in Foxholm, and holding by the other hand little Ozzy, who exulted less in his new velvet cap and tunic than in the notion that he was bridesman to Tin-Tin.

Last of all came a couple whom the villagers eyed yet more eagerly than the bride and bridegroom: a fine old gentleman, who looked round with keen glances that cowed the conscious scapegraces among them, and a stately lady in blue-and-white silk robes, who must surely be like Queen Charlotte.[35]

'Well, that theer's whut I coal a pictur,' said old 'Mester' Ford, a true Staffordshire patriarch, who leaned on a stick and held his head very much on one side, with the air of a man who had little hope of the present generation, but would at all events give it the benefit of his criticism. 'Th' yoong men noo-a-deys, the're poor squashy things – the' looke well anoof, but the' woon't wear, the' woon't wear. Theer's ne'er un'll carry his 'ears like that Sir Cris'fer Chuvrell.'

'Ull bet ye two pots,' said another of the seniors, 'as that yoongster a-walkin' wi' th' parson's wife 'll be Sir Cris'fer's son – he fevours him.'

'Nay, yae'll bet that wi' as big a fule as yersen; hae's noo son at all. As I oonderstan', hae's the nevey as is' t' heir th' esteate. The coochman as puts oop at th' White Hoss tellt me as theer war another nevey, a deal finer chap t' looke at nor this un, as died in a fit, all on a soodden, an' soo this here yoong un's got upo' th' perch istid.'

At the church gate Mr Bates was standing in a new suit, ready to speak words of good omen as the bride and bridegroom approached. He had come all the way from Cheverel Manor on purpose to see Miss Tina happy once more, and would have been in a state of unmixed joy but for the inferiority of the wedding nosegays to what he could have furnished from the garden at the Manor.

'God A'maighty bless ye both, an' send ye long laife an' happiness,' were the good gardener's rather tremulous words.

'Thank you, uncle Bates; always remember Tina,' said the sweet low voice, which fell on Mr Bates's ear for the last time.

The wedding journey was to be a circuitous route to Shepperton, where Mr Gilfil had been for several months inducted as vicar. This small living had been given him through the interest of an old friend who had some claim on the gratitude of the Oldinport family, and it was a satisfaction both to Maynard and Sir Christopher that a home to which he might take Caterina had thus readily presented itself at a distance from Cheverel Manor. For it had never yet been thought safe that she should revisit the scene of her sufferings, her health continuing too delicate to encourage the slightest risk of painful excitement. In a year or two, perhaps, by the time old Mr Crichley, the rector of Cumbermoor, should have left a world of gout, and when Caterina would very likely be a happy mother, Maynard might safely take up his abode at Cumbermoor, and Tina would feel nothing but content at seeing a new 'little black-eyed monkey' running up and down the gallery and gardens of the Manor. A mother dreads no memories – those shadows have all melted away in the dawn of baby's smile.

In these hopes, and in the enjoyment of Tina's nestling affection, Mr Gilfil tasted a few months of perfect happiness. She had come to lean entirely on his love, and to find life sweet for his sake. Her continual languor and want of active interest was a natural consequence of bodily feebleness, and the prospect of her becoming a mother was a new ground for hoping the best. But the delicate plant had been too deeply bruised, and in the struggle to put forth a blossom it died.

Tina died, and Maynard Gilfil's love went with her into deep silence for evermore.


## EPILOGUE

This was Mr Gilfil's love story, which lay far back from the time when he sat, worn and grey, by his lonely fireside in Shepperton Vicarage. Rich brown locks, passionate love, and deep early sorrow, strangely different as they seem from the scanty white hairs, the apathetic content, and the unexpectant quiescence of old age, are but part of the same life's journey; as the bright Italian plains, with the sweet *Addio*[36] of their beckoning maidens, are part of the same day's travel that brings us to the other side of the mountain, between the sombre rocky walls and among the guttural voices of the Valais.

To those who were familiar only with the grey-haired vicar, jogging leisurely along on his old chestnut cob, it would perhaps have been hard to believe that he had ever been the Maynard Gilfil who, with a heart full of passion and tenderness, had urged his black Kitty to her swiftest gallop on the way to Callam, or that the old gentleman of caustic tongue, and bucolic tastes, and sparing habits, had known all the deep secrets of devoted love, had struggled through its days and nights of anguish, and trembled under its unspeakable joys.

And indeed the Mr Gilfil of those late Shepperton days had more of the knots and ruggedness of poor human nature than there lay any clear hint of in the open-eyed loving Maynard. But it is with men as with trees: if you lop off their finest branches, into which they were pouring their young life-juice, the wounds will be healed over with some rough boss, some odd excrescence, and what might have been a grand tree expanding into liberal shade, is but a whimsical misshapen trunk. Many an irritating fault, many an unlovely oddity, has come of a hard sorrow, which has crushed and maimed the nature just when it was expanding into plenteous beauty; and the trivial erring life that we visit with our harsh blame, may be but as the unsteady motion of a man whose best limb is withered.

And so the dear old Vicar, though he had something of the knotted whimsical character of the poor lopped oak, had yet been sketched out by nature as a noble tree. The heart of him was sound, the grain was of the finest, and in the grey-haired man who filled his pocket with sugar-plums for the little children, whose most biting words were directed against the evil-doing of the rich man, and who, with all his social pipes and slipshod talk, never sank below the highest level of his parishioners' respect, there was the main trunk of the same brave, faithful, tender nature that had poured out the finest, freshest forces of its life-current in a first and only love – the love of Tina.

# NOTES

1. Boeotia bordered Athens in ancient Greece; its inhabitants were portrayed as backward compared to their Athenian neighbours.

2. Lambs after their first shearing.

3. The New Testament's Gallio was a proconsul who refused to judge the dispute between Paul and the Jews in Corinth (Acts 18:12–15).

4. Fully 'false front', a partial wig that covers the the front of the head.

5. Sir Joshua Reynolds (1723–92), celebrated portrait painter.

6. Antoine Watteau (1684–1721), French painter.

7. Antinous (c.110–130 AD) was a youth of renowned beauty and lover of the Emperor Hadrian; he was deified after his death.

8 During the Thirty Years' War Magdeburg was besieged by the Holy Roman Empire's imperial troops.

9. Il Guercino (1591–1666), Italian painter.

10. Diminutive of *padrone*, 'master' (Italian).

11. '*Ho perduto il bel sembiante*' ('I have lost the fair face') is a song from Giovanni Paesiello's (1740–1816) cantata *Amor Vendicato*.

12. A card game for two players.

13. 'What am I to do without Eurydice?' (Italian) is a song from German composer Christoph Gluck's (1714–87) *Orfeo ed Euridice* (1762).

14. *Les Amours du chevalier de Faublas* by Jean-Baptiste Louvet de Couvray (1760–97).

15. Jean Jacques Rousseau (1712–78), French philospher and essayist, supported himself at one stage in his life by 'copying music at so much a page' (French).

16. Poor man (Italian).

17. Lady's maid.

18. Italy.

19 First tenor (Italian).

20. Affectionate term for a small child (Italian).

21. Most excellent woman (Italian).

22. 'Here is the most noble woman' (Italian).

23. From Sophocles' play *Ajax*.

24. It is in fact Friar Roger Bacon (1214–94) who was credited by some to have invented gunpowder. Sir Francis Bacon was made Baron Verulam in 1618, hence the reference three lines later.

25. At pleasure (Latin).

26. A cured tobacco, produced in Latakia, Syria.

27. Glance (French).

28. By virtue of one's official position (Latin).

29. In 1666 an Act of Parliament was passed that required people to bury their dead dressed in wool; it was designed to encourage the manufacture of woolen goods. The Act was unpopular, people preferring to follow the earlier custom of burying the dead dressed

in linen, but the Act wasn't repealed until 1814.

30. 'The unlucky gift of beauty' (Italian), a quotation from the Italian poet Vincenzo da Filicaja's 'Sonnet to Italy'.

31. John Tillotson (1630–94) was Archbishop of Canterbury from 1691 to 1694.

32. Small bottle of smelling salts.

33. Feeble (dialect word).

34. Toga of manhood (Latin).

35. Queen Charlotte (1744–1818), wife of King George III.

36. Goodbye (Italian).

# BIOGRAPHICAL NOTE

George Eliot was born Mary Ann Evans in Warwickshire in 1819. The youngest daughter of Robert Evans (a land agent) and Christina Pearson, she was a deeply religious child, and taught at Sunday school from the age of twelve. In 1828 she was sent to school in Nuneaton where she came under the influence of various Evangelicals, including the Revd John Edmund Jones, a preacher who would later appear in a number of her novels.

Following her mother's death in 1836, Mary Ann (now Marian) became her father's housekeeper and companion, but continued to educate herself in her spare time. In 1841 she moved to Coventry and became acquainted with the religious freethinkers Charles and Caroline Bray. Their influence on her caused her to question – and reject – much of her evangelical heritage, but the role of religion remained important to her and featured in many of her later works. Through the Brays, Marian was commissioned to translate Strauss's *Life of Jesus*, which appeared, anonymously, in 1846. As a result of this she met the publisher John Chapman who gave her a position on the *Westminster Review* in 1851. Around this time she moved to London and formed close friendships first with Herbert Spencer, who found her intimidating, and then with George Henry Lewes, with whom she lived until his death in 1878. The two never married as Lewes had previously married and had never divorced.

'The Sad Fortunes of the Reverend Amos Barton', the first of her *Scenes of Clerical Life*, appeared in *Blackwell's Magazine* in 1857 under the authorship of George Eliot; this was closely followed by 'Mr Gilfil's Love Story' and 'Janet's Repentance'. These were widely praised but speculation surrounded the identity of George Eliot, many supposing 'him' to be a clergyman. After much conjecture, she eventually stepped forward and revealed her identity.

*Adam Bede* appeared in 1859 and established her as a leading novelist of the day. This she followed up with *The Mill on the Floss* (1860) and *Silas Marner* (1861). *Middlemarch*, considered by many to be her masterpiece, was published in instalments in 1871–2, and *Daniel Deronda* in 1874–6. With these behind her, she was hailed as the greatest living novelist, and counted Henry James, Ralph Waldo Emerson, Ivan Turgenev and Queen Victoria among her admirers.

In 1878 Lewes died and Eliot formed a new attachment, marrying the forty-year-old John Walter Cross in 1880. This relationship distressed many of her friends, but brought about reconciliation with her brother Isaac with whom she had been estranged since 1857. Not long after her marriage, however, she died and, in 1882, was buried alongside Lewes.